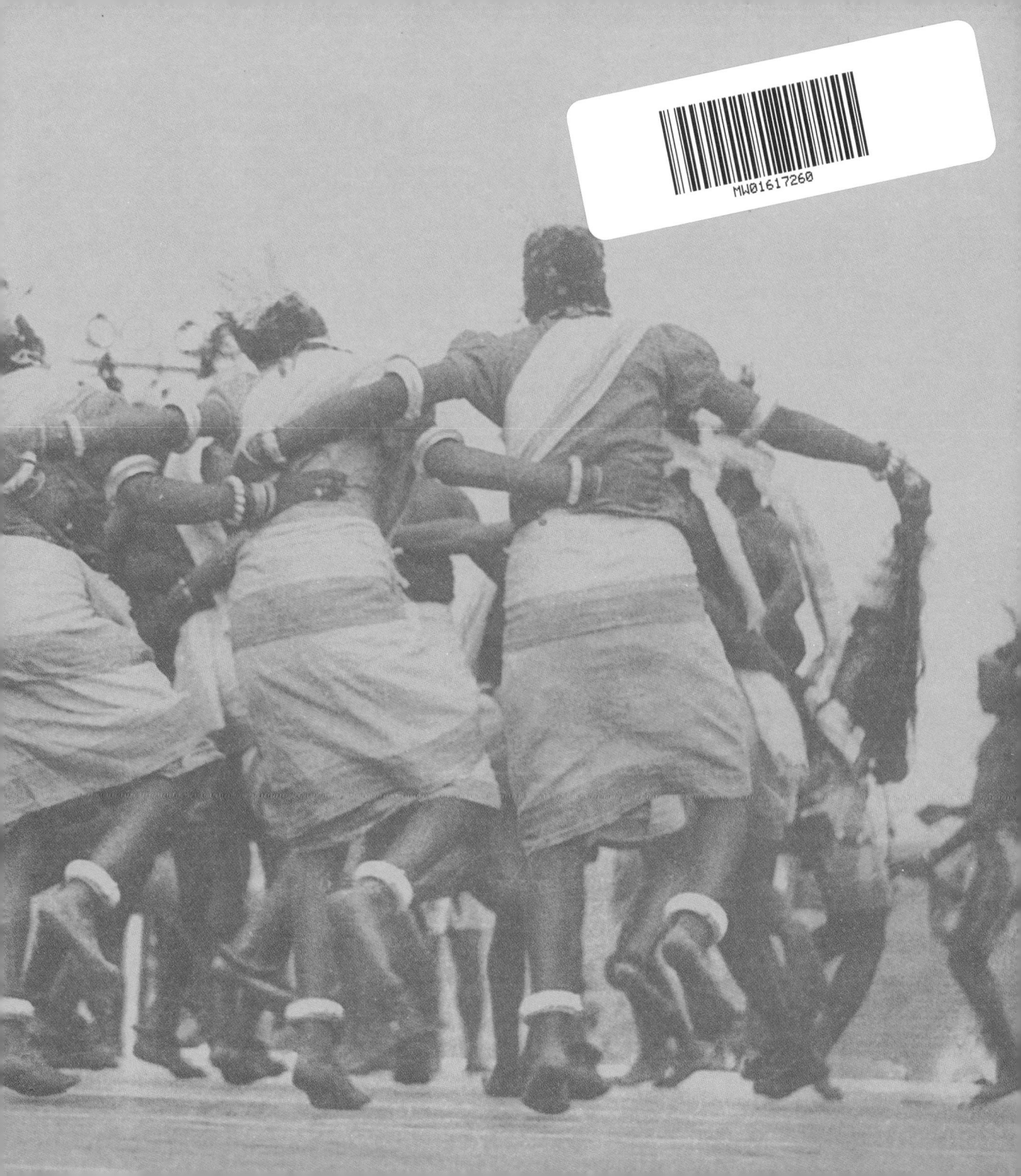

FOLK DANCE

TRIBAL, RITUAL & MARTIAL FORMS

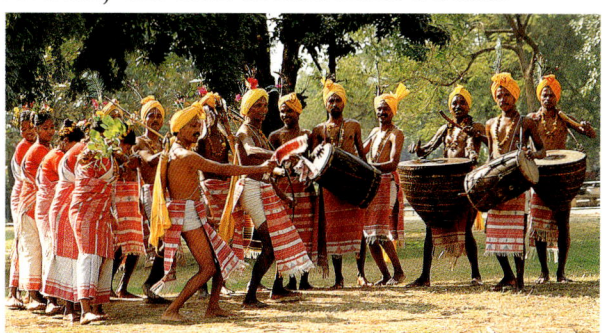

Published 2003 by

Rupa & Co

7/16, Ansari Road, Daryaganj
New Delhi 110 002

Sales Centres:

Allahabad Bangalore Chandigarh Chennai
Dehradun Hyderabad Jaipur Kathmandu
Kolkata Ludhiana Mumbai Pune

Book Design & Typeset by
Arrt Creations
45 Nehru Apts Kalkaji
New Delhi 110 019

Copy Editing: Kohinoor Dasgupta/Jacaranda

Printed in India by
Ajanta Offset & Packagings Ltd. New Delhi

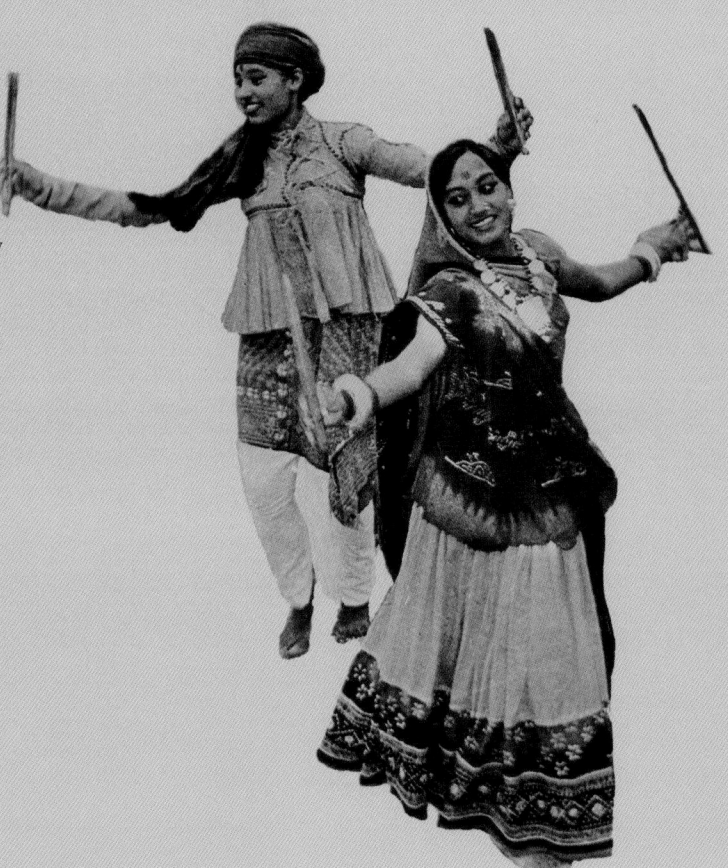

FOLK DANCE
TRIBAL, RITUAL & MARTIAL FORMS

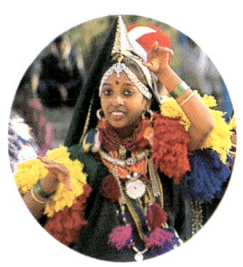

Ashish Mohan Khokar

Rupa & Co

ETERNAL INDIA

DEDICATION

In memory of the late K. Shekharan Panikar,
who had a genius for the arts creating something out of nothing,
somewhat like the spirited open-hearted folk dancers of India.

And for Yog Sunder, born a prince but at heart, a son of the soil.

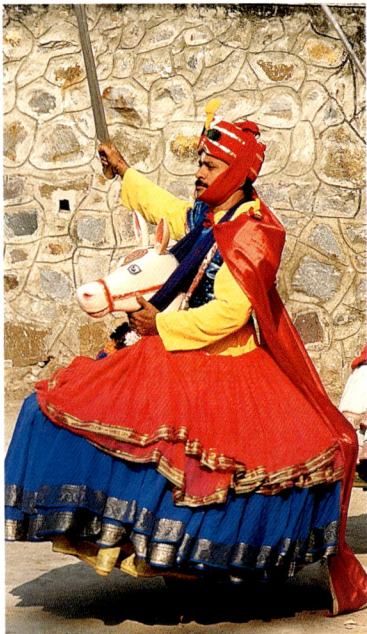

PHOTO CREDITS

B/W: Mohan Khokar Dance Archives of India
Colour: Ashish Mohan Khokar

CONTENTS

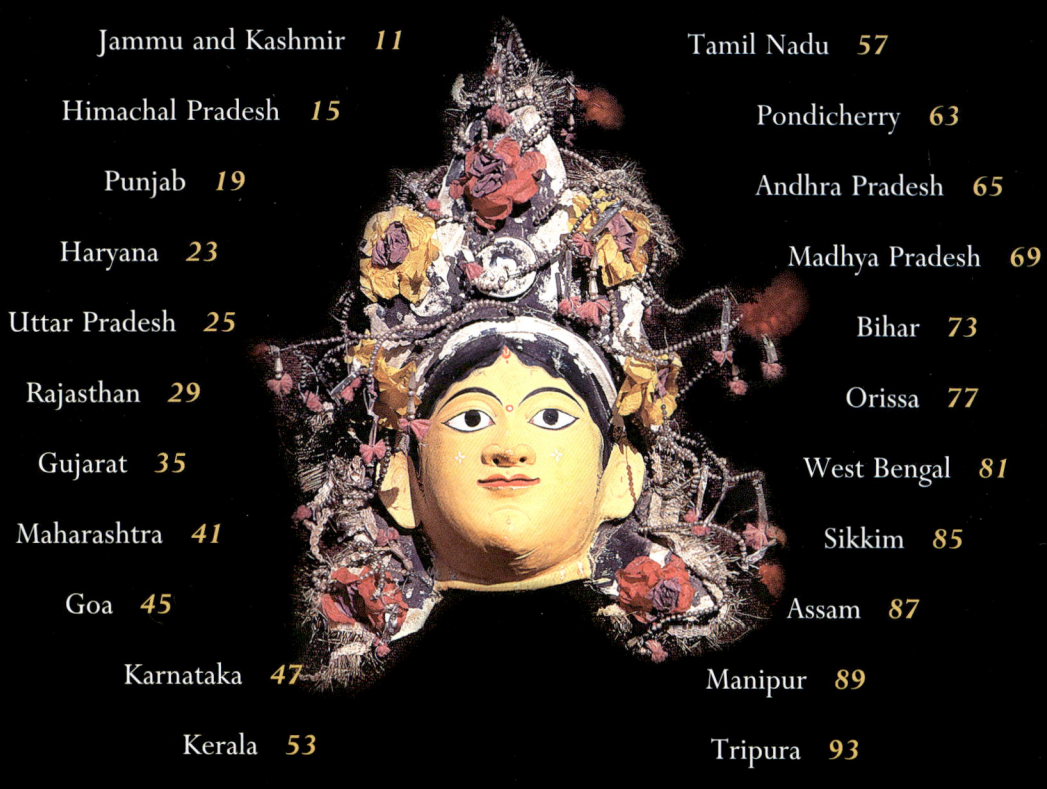

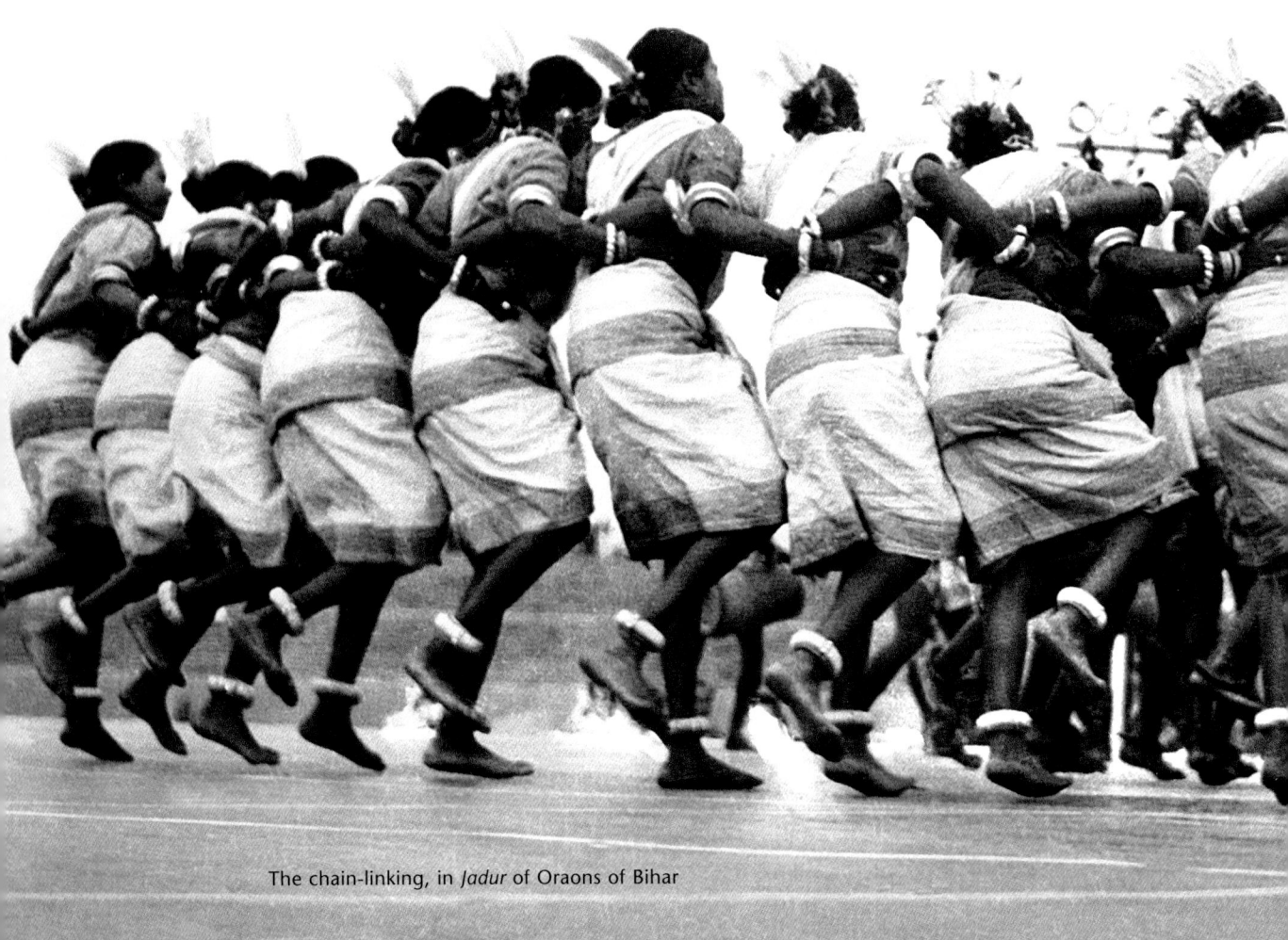

The chain-linking, in *Jadur* of Oraons of Bihar

INTRODUCTION

India dances to the rhythms of a million rural feet. Without formal training in dance, unaware of classical traditions, mostly unlettered and totally unfettered, the innocent dancers of the villages of India dance because they must. There is no reason for their dance, except a desire to celebrate life. Unlike dancers rigorously groomed in the classical genres, the folk dancers have no agenda of attaining glory or greatness, no hope of awards or rewards, no experience of commendations or adulations. They dance because they are meant to.

Like most folk cultures around the world, the folk traditions of India, too, encompass a great variety of occasions and events to celebrate. Farmers and agricultural workers practically have a dance to welcome every seasonal change. They dance with joyous abandon to create for themselves their raison d'être – a reinstatement of the beliefs rooted in the mythology of their land and culture.

Nothing is for effect. Their dance is not staged. There is no formal platform, except for the vast scenic theatre of open fields or a riverbank – or just a village square. Men, women, and children, the young and the old alike, participate in the dance of joy. They believe that their dance is a kind of prayer to Nature and its puissant gods, a prayer that invokes and propitiates, as well as gives thanks. They dance not for an audience, but for themselves.

The folk dancers comprise a large segment of India's populace, which otherwise has no connection to or background in dancing. Hard working and not very affluent , the rural folk form the nucleus of the village economy. And in their everyday lives they weave a tapestry of song and dance at birth and death, marriage and festival.

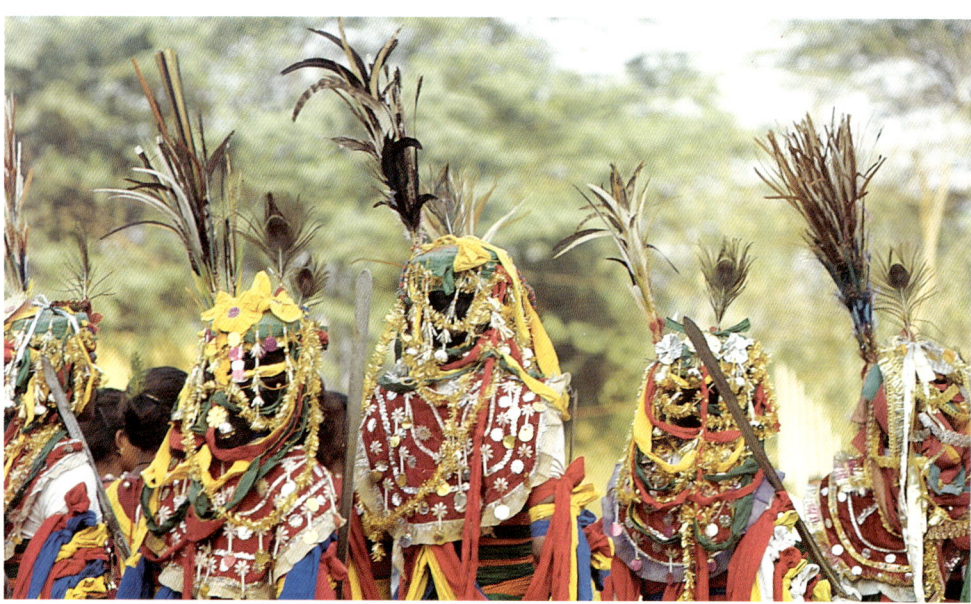

Bheels, Gujarat

It is said that for such a large country as India, there are far too few classical dance forms. True, but this paucity is easily offset by the abundant variety of folk dances in virtually all nooks and crannies of the country. There are over a hundred forms of folk dances in India, with regional variations. Everywhere, ranging from hamlets tucked into the rugged Himalayan foothills in the north, the lush plains of the Gangetic belt, the estuaries of the east, the valleys of the west, and the riverbanks of the south, folk dancing takes place throughout the year. It needs no promotion or projection. It is simply a happy, vigorous ode to life and living.

In independent India, there has been a large-scale migration of people from the villages to the cities. Urbanisation has brought the erstwhile villagers in touch with city glamour, consumerism, the rat race, educational degrees, politics, cinema, and television. These urban influences are steadily seeping into Indian villages, alienating the simple folk from their traditional moorings while often doing nothing to improve their quality of life in terms of basic needs. But in the process, the rest of the country has come to know of these innocent, rustic people to whom dance is not an act or public performance but a part of life itself. In their folk dances lies India's traditional essence.

This book is an attempt to take you on a rhythmic journey through the different states of India and catch the beats of Indian folk culture.

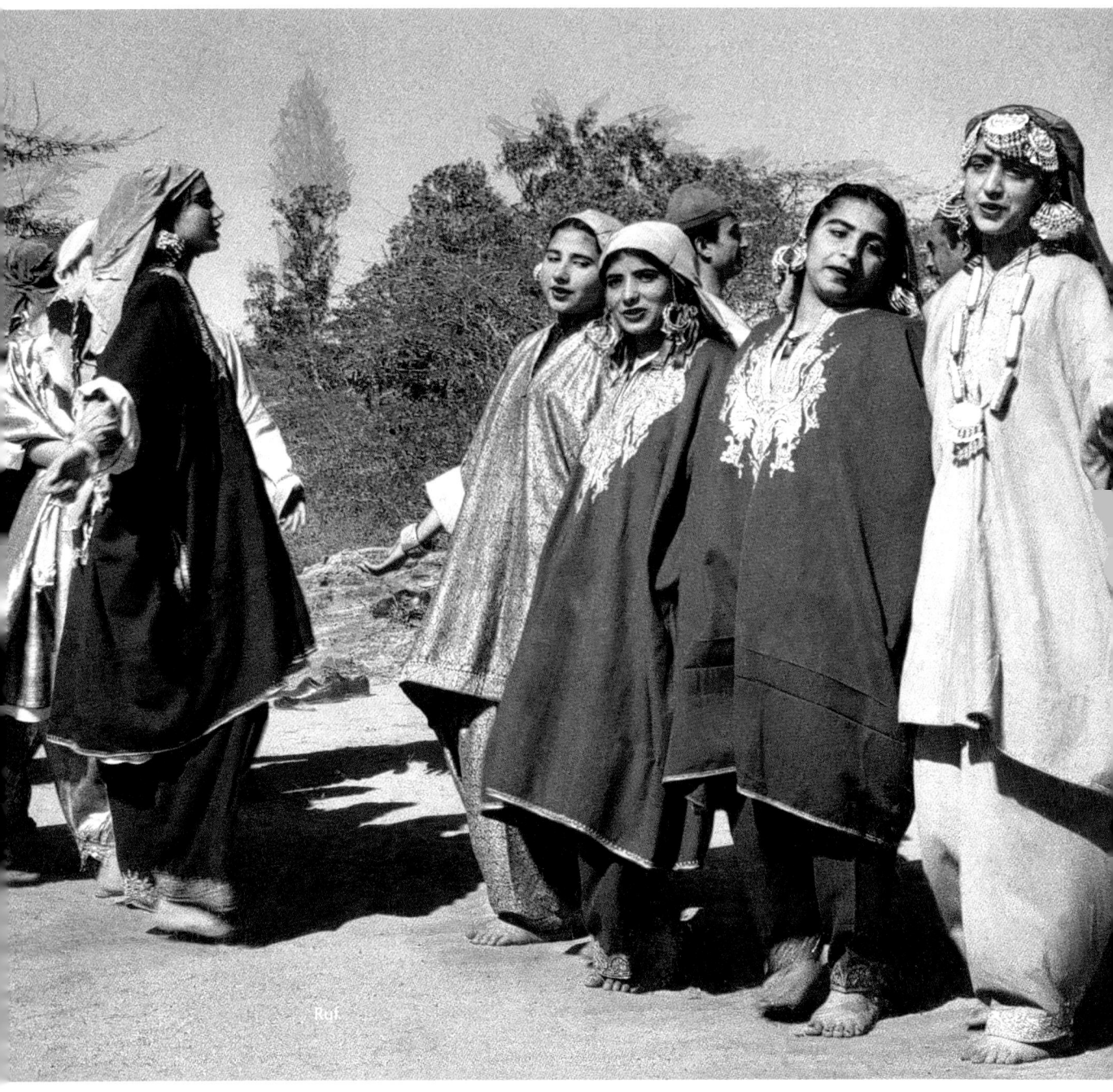

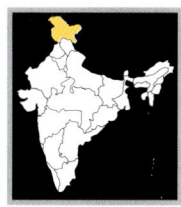

o n e

Jammu and Kashmir

ur journey starts at the foothills of the Himalayas, in Jammu
and Kashmir, the Indian state that used to be described as a
paradise on earth. Despite the difficult terrain and unfriendly
climate and conditions, the people of Kashmir, fair of heart as well
as skin, have always found the time and motivation for art. Their
beautiful land and rich cultural heritage are sources of inspiration
for them. This region comprises areas peopled by several self-
contained ethno-religious units. Ladakh, for instance, is inhabited
predominantly by Buddhists, Kashmir by Muslims, and Jammu by
Hindus. For centuries, the people of the region succeeded in co-
existing and making their composite folk customs overcome the
divisions of creeds and castes.

As rural Jammu and Kashmir is traditionally a conservative society in which women and men do not normally interact in public, even on social occasions, the folk dances of the state reflect this gender separation.

Ruf is a dance form performed by Kashmiri women on festive and religious occasions. It has simple steps; the dancers face each other in two rows, singing songs of love and heroism while moving and swaying backward and forward.

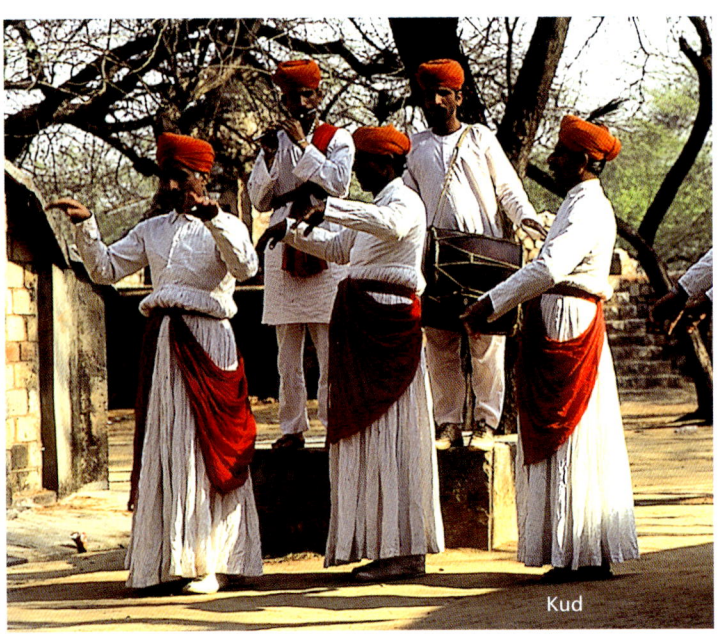

Kud

Kud is performed by men belonging to the Dogra community of Jammu. Handsome and fine-featured, these dancers look disciplined and dignified as they form a ring and dance the *Kud*. Their bodies bend and straighten in recurrent, measured steps. They maintain an even and easy tempo.

Hikat, danced by women, is an adaptation of a game that children play, wherein they hold hands and form a delirious human merry-go-round. With feet firmly planted and hands twined, pairs of dancers sing, swirl, and laugh in a display of sheer exuberance.

Bacha Nagma is a dance performed by boys dressed as girls, and reflects the influence of the Kathak style. Long skirts and veils adorn the boys, who sing while they dance. This ceremonial folk form is commonly performed at weddings.

Dumhal is danced by men of the Wattal community in the interior reaches of Kashmir. It is performed by dancers togged out in a costume of tunic, long shirt and a pointed cap. Nowadays, the traditional costume is often teamed with a pair of canvas shoes to make for a more athletic and agile performance!

Bhand Pather is a form of folk theatre portraying the oppression suffered by the Kashmiris down the centuries. Part-mime, part-dance, it draws upon Kashmiri, Dogri, and Punjabi literature for material. Masks are used to represent animals.

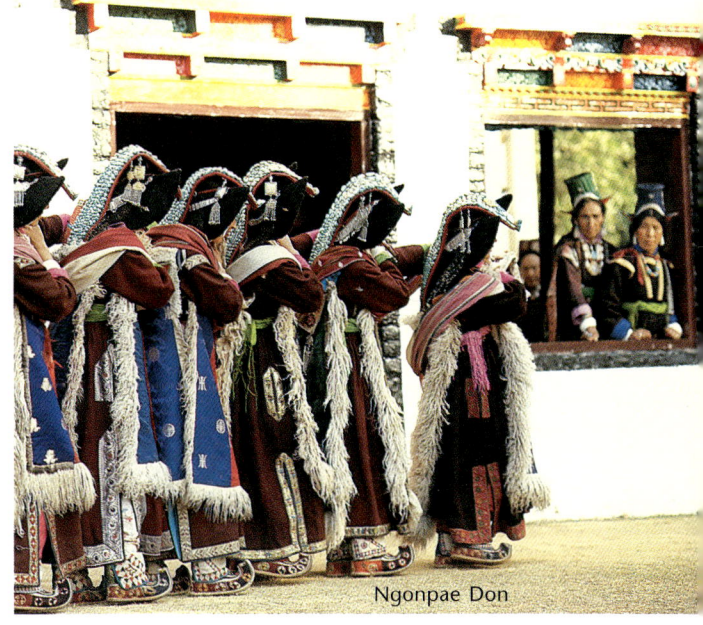
Ngonpae Don

Ngonpae Don is the most popular of the dances of the Buddhists of Ladakh. The dances are didactic in nature and not meant for entertainment. The lamas or monks who perform the dance don masks representing various evil spirits and forces. Thus, they look frightening although the accompanying music and the overall mood of the dance is gentle.

Nati

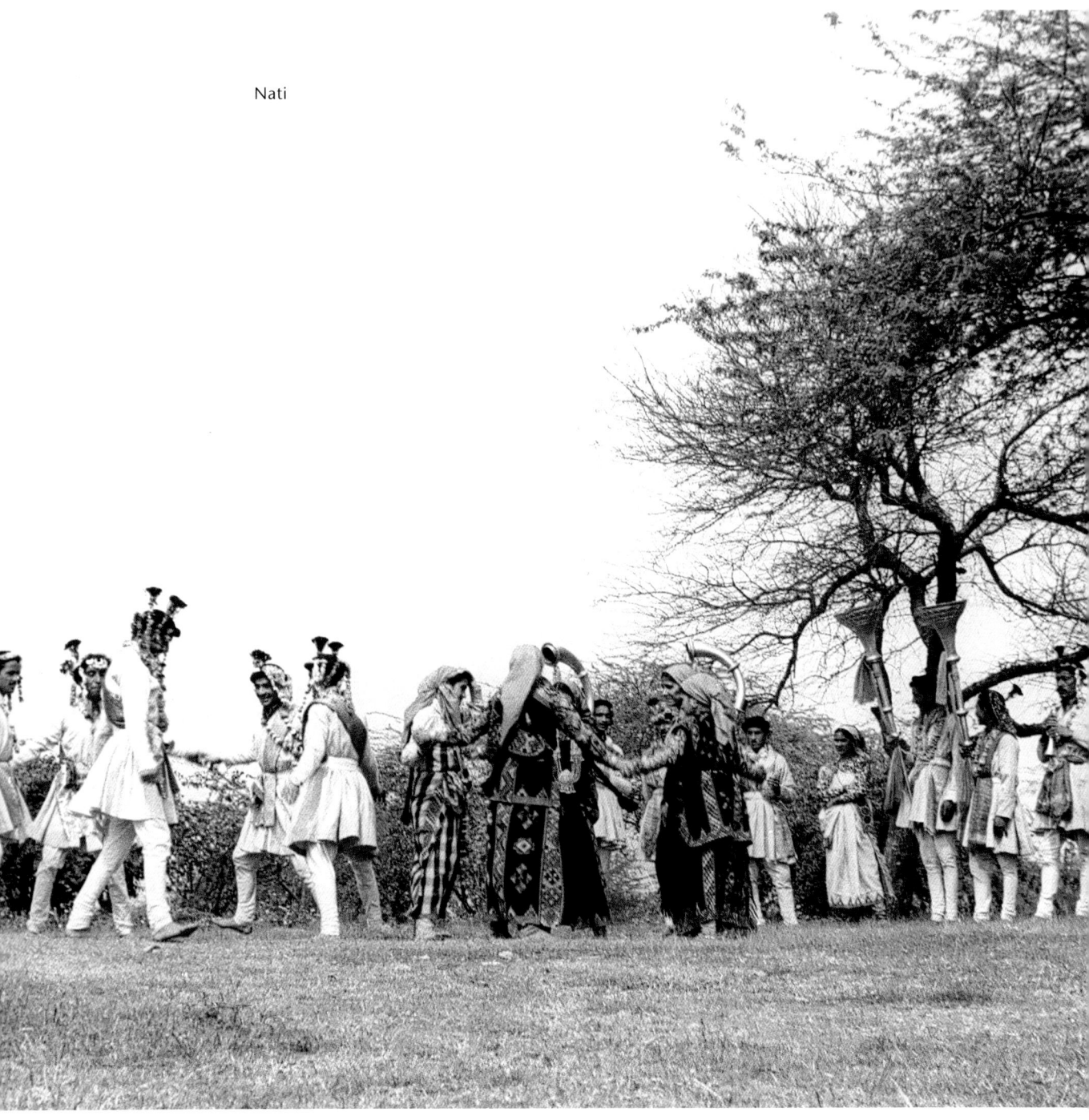

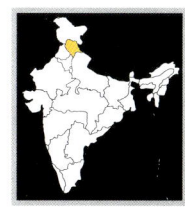

t w o

HIMACHAL PRADESH

*F*or the beauty of both its people and its scenery, Himachal Pradesh is indeed god's gift to mankind. At once gentle and genteel, spirited and spiritual, its inhabitants need little or no excuse to sing and dance. At weddings, feasts, fairs, sowings, and harvests they revel in the beauty of their land, matched only by their own. The Himachalis love their land and the abundant gifts it gives not only to them, but to the entire country. Himachal Pradesh is the Fruit Bowl of India. Living in the recesses of the Himalayan ranges, these rugged but refined people are attuned to their environment and habitat. Various gods and goddesses are worshipped, but none more than Mother Earth. Local potentates and the people come together to participate in the grand Dussehra festival held in this state. This festival, in fact, witnesses one of the largest annual folk gatherings in India, with tens of thousands assembling to propitiate the gods of the valleys through music and dance.

Singhi is a dance of Lahaul-Spiti, a region in Himachal Pradesh that remains snowbound for most parts of the year. The tale of the Snow-Lion ('Singhi'), which stands for peace and prosperity, is of paramount importance for the hill people of these parts.

Gaddi

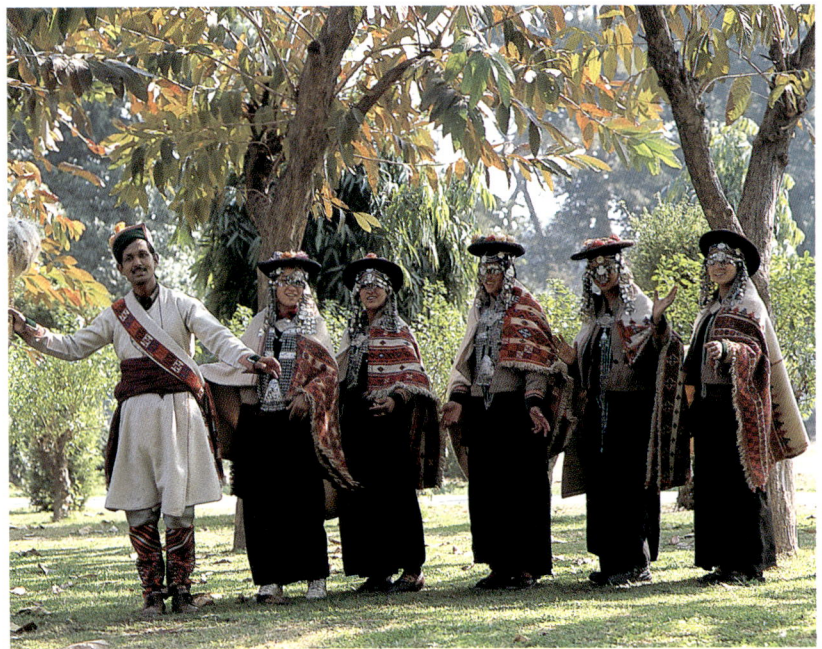

The **Gaddi** peasants of the Chamba region perform their dance, which often coincides with or is the culmination point of the July-August Minjar fair. Both men and women participate in this lively dance.

Parasa highlights the plight of Parasurama's mother, Renuka. The lake Renuka is so named after the legend of Renuka, who was killed by Parasurama, the axe-wielding incarnation of Vishnu. The dance has a martial character.

Nati is a dance of Kulu, a region well known for its smiling people and miles of apple orchards. During the Dussehra festival, idols of Raghunathji are brought from different shrines to the valley of Kulu, and much singing and dancing takes place.

Kinnauri is a representative dance of the Kinnaur region of Himachal Pradesh. It is performed by a close-knit group of men and women dressed in their colourful daily attire. Drums, cymbals, and trumpets form the musical accompaniment to this revelry.

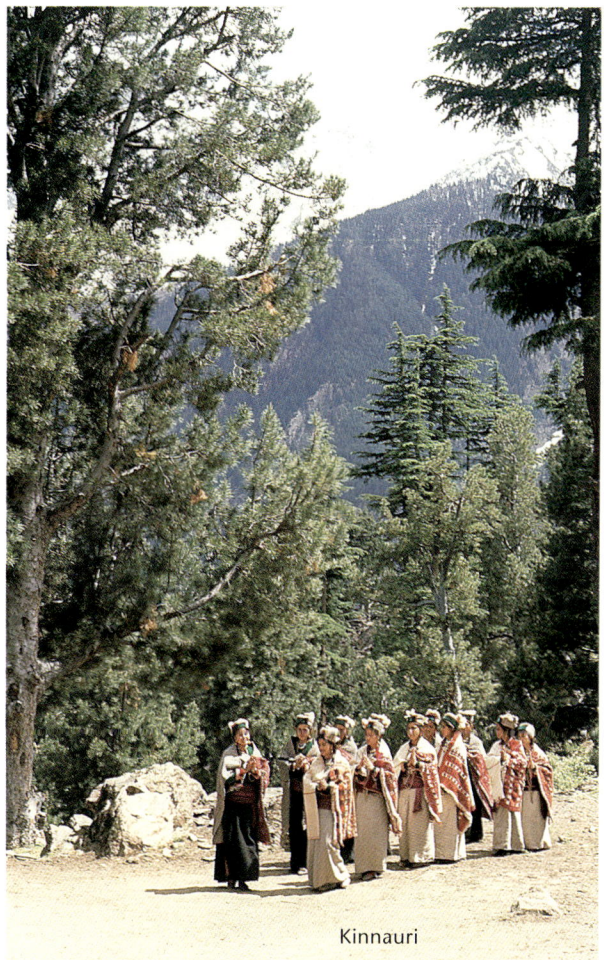
Kinnauri

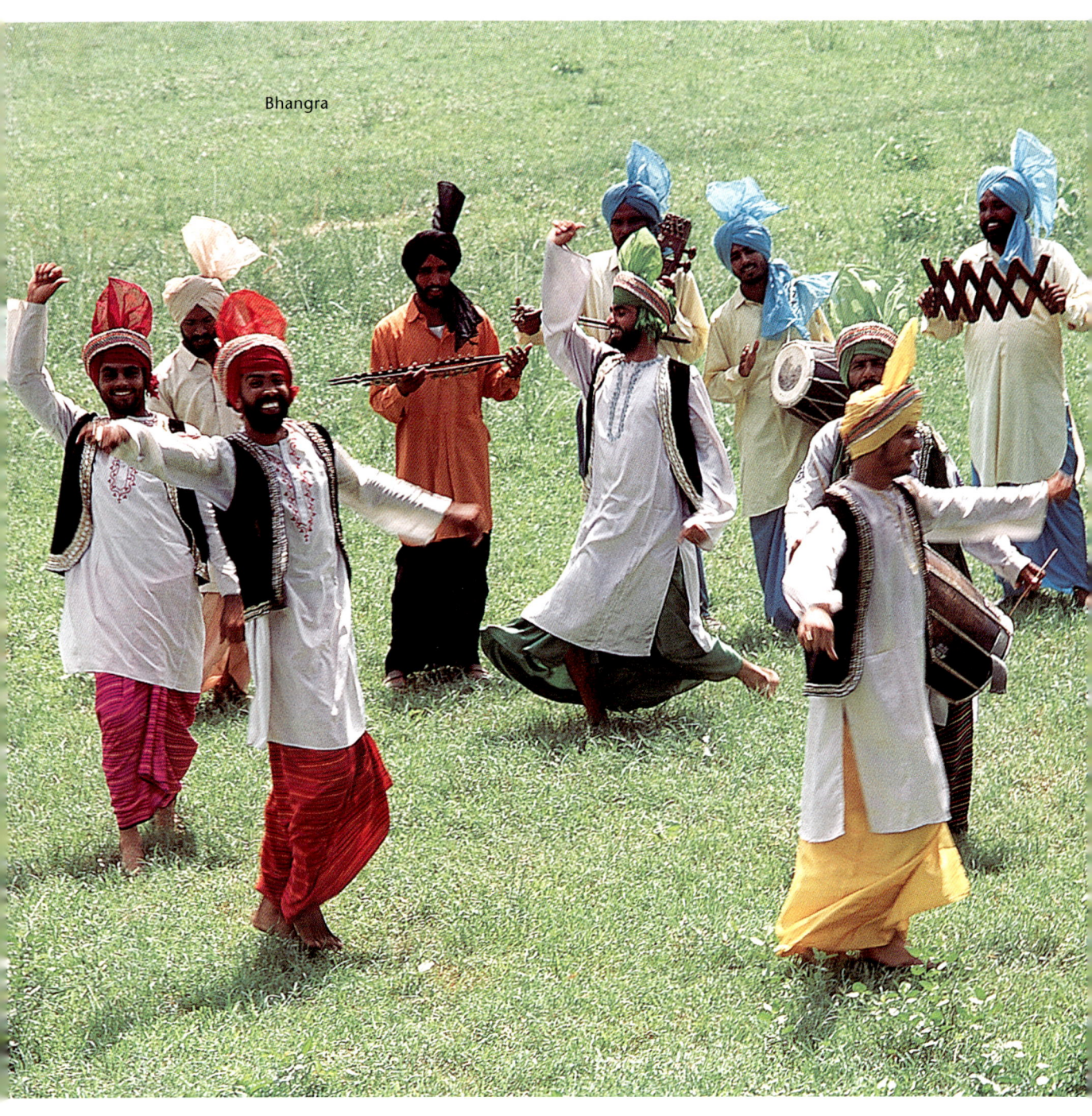
Bhangra

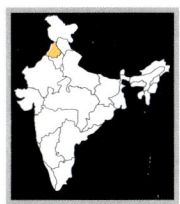

t h r e e

PUNJAB

The dances of Punjab are earthy and robust, just like its people. The land of five rivers (Sutlej, Beas, Rabi, Chenab and Jhelum), Punjab, has given to India a race that is daring and noble. The Punjabis symbolise freedom of spirit and daredevilry. They regard dancing as their birthright, and their dances reflect this attitude of supreme confidence and conviviality. The people are capable of strenuous work, yet nothing seems to sap them of their infectious zest for life. They do nothing by halves. So they launch into their dances too with swaggering gusto and overflowing energy.

Bhangra gives this Indian state its very identity. Performed by men, this folk style has jumps, leaps, swirls, skips, and hops – just about any physical feat that a virile son-of-the-soil can attempt. It is punctuated by a lot of acrobatics, meant to showcase daredevilry.

Clapping, snapping of the fingers, and a recitation of *boli* (witty couplets) are its specialities. Shiny short jackets are worn over loose shirts that are paired with flowing *lungis* and a huge, crimped, fancy turban. Bhangra is danced to the accompaniment of drums and cymbals.

Hola Mohalla is the dance of baptism by Sikhs who join the Khalsa *Panth* (order) and denotes the martial traits of the Sikhs. Attendants and priests take out a procession replete with swords, knives, battons, sticks and spears on the occasion of Baishakhi and Sankranti.

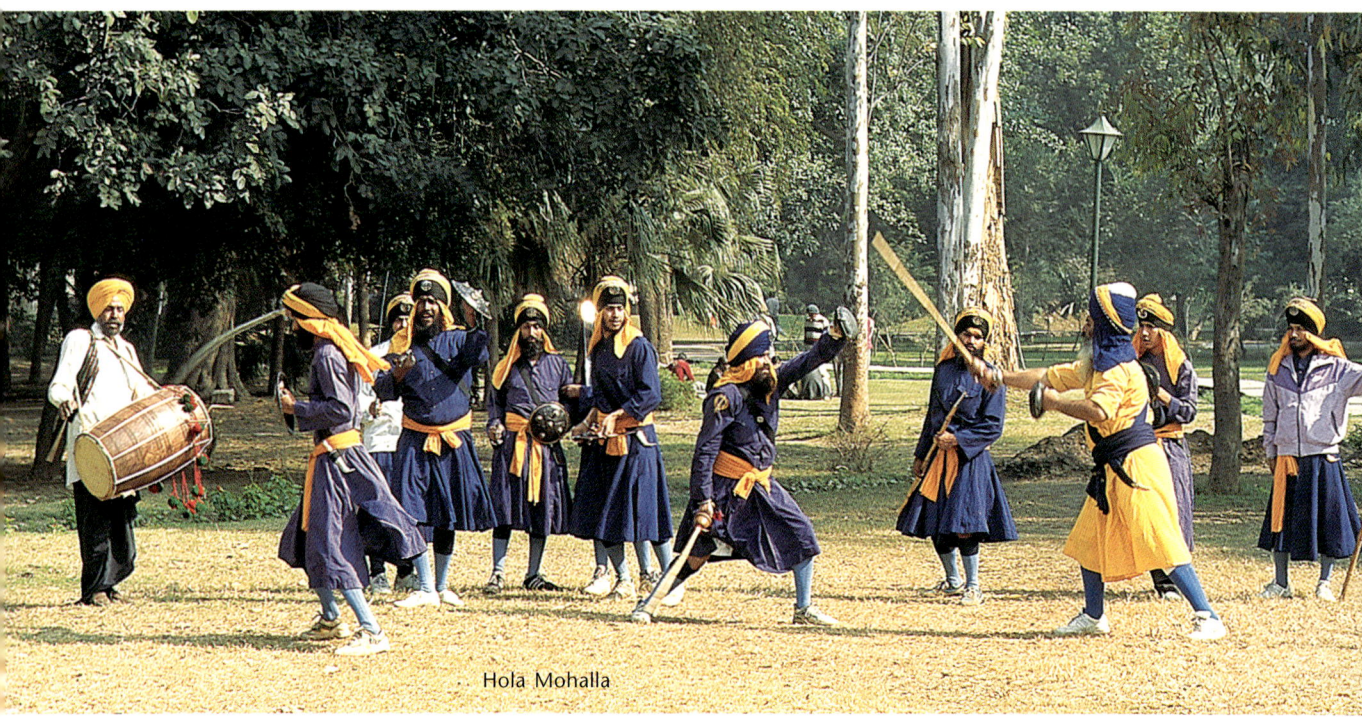

Hola Mohalla

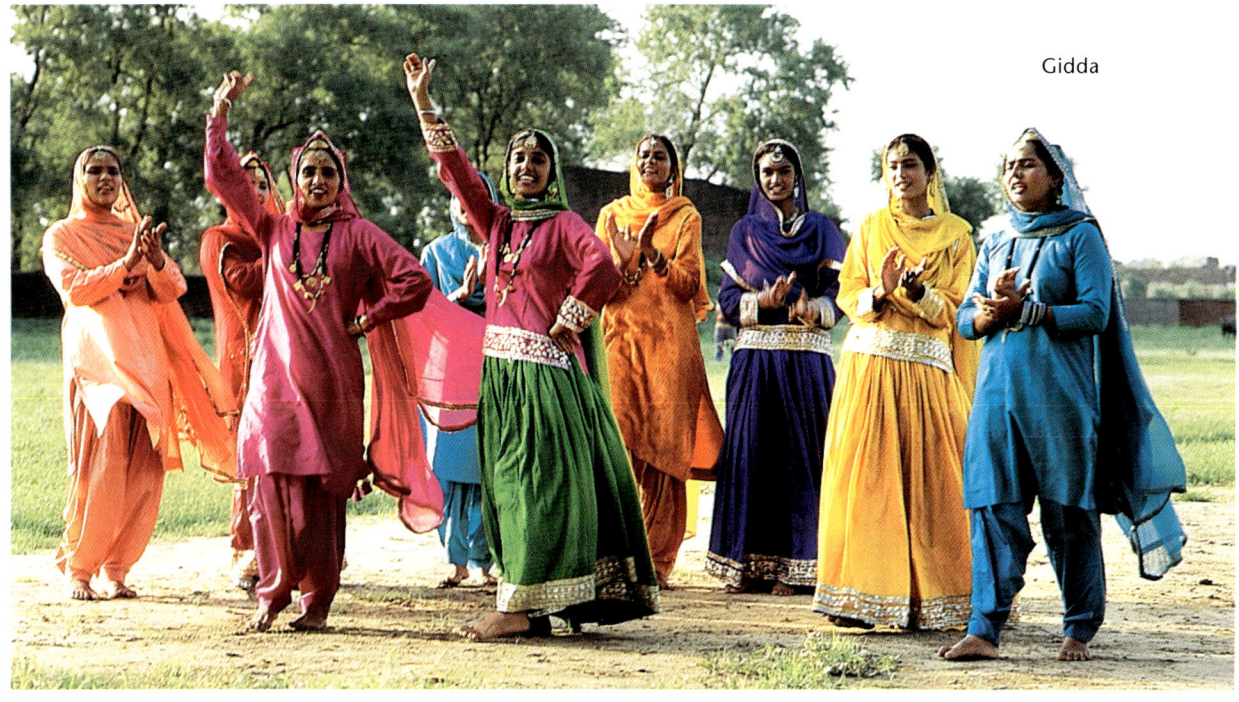

Gidda

Gidda is the feminine riposte to Bhangra, no less colourful or vigorous. The dancers look resplendent in their wedding finery. *Gidda* can be danced by a group, by pairs of women, solo or in any other convenient combination. An interesting aspect of this dance is that occasionally a dancer comes out of the group and dances on her own while the others continue to sway and clap.

Kikli is a part of the Gidda but in this dance, like in the Hikat dance style of Kashmir, women pair up, join hands, and whirl around. A great deal of school girlish shrieking and laughter adds to the enjoyment. The festival of Teeyan, which welcomes the rains, is the principal occasion for this folk dance.

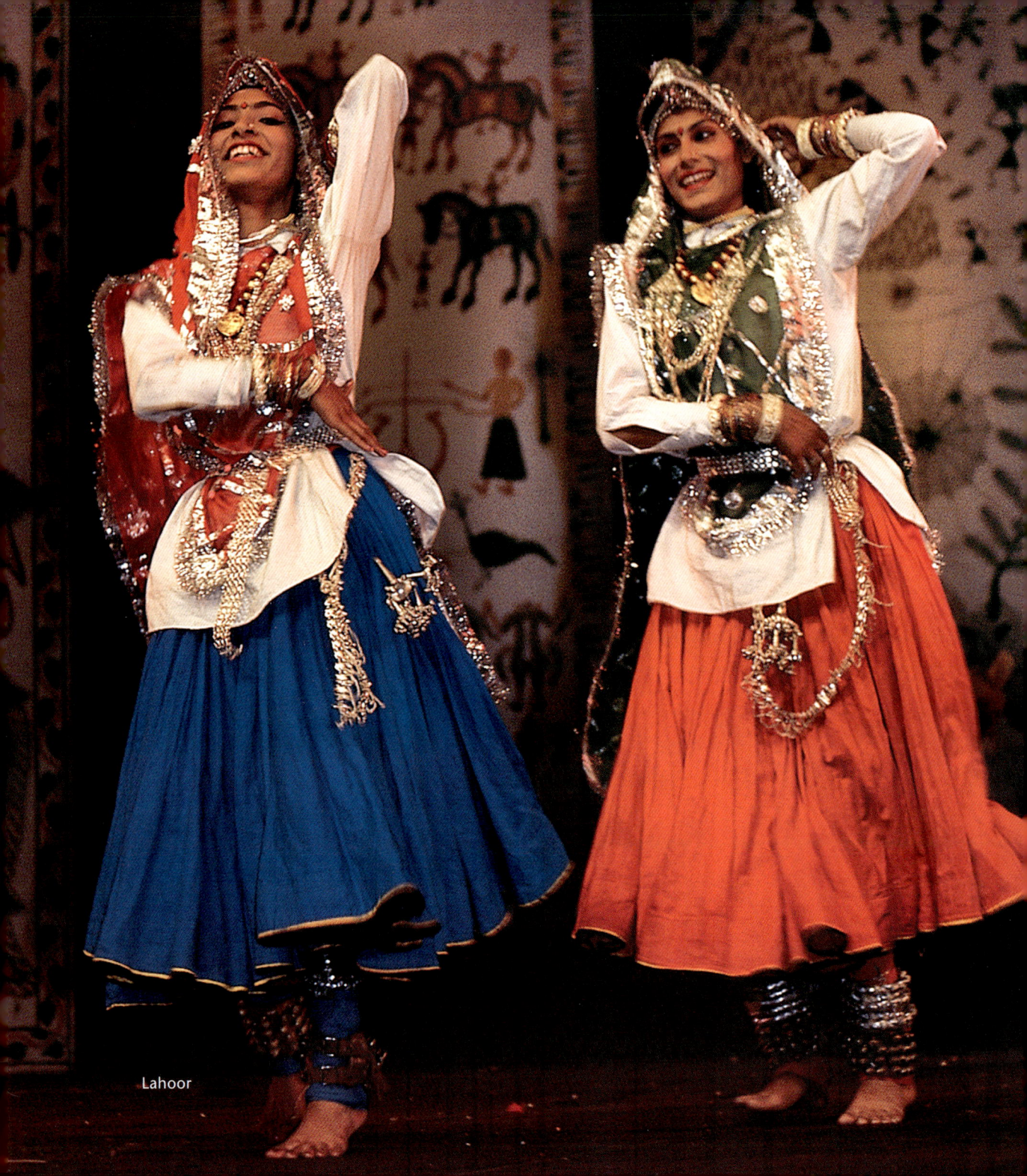
Lahoor

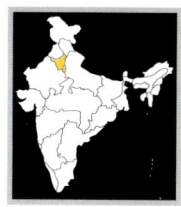

f o u r

HARYANA

Haryana, which is the Jat land of North India and the grain bowl of the region, has its own quota of mirth and merry-making. Not given to public display of emotion, the tall, lean Haryanvis celebrate their seasons in a manner befitting their robust, sedate personalities.

Dhamyal is the main dance of the state. It is performed to the beat of a drum called Duph, which is circular and at least three feet in diameter. It gives a flat rhythmic note, to which several feet, adorned with jingling ankle bells, keep the beat, providing a pleasing sound effect. Men sing and play the instruments. It is the women who dance, clapping their hands.

Lahoor is the principal dance of the women of Haryana. It is performed in spring, when there is plenty of work in the fields and dancing provides a welcome opportunity to relax. Sometimes the men do join in, especially when the women weave witty questions into their song to goad them on!

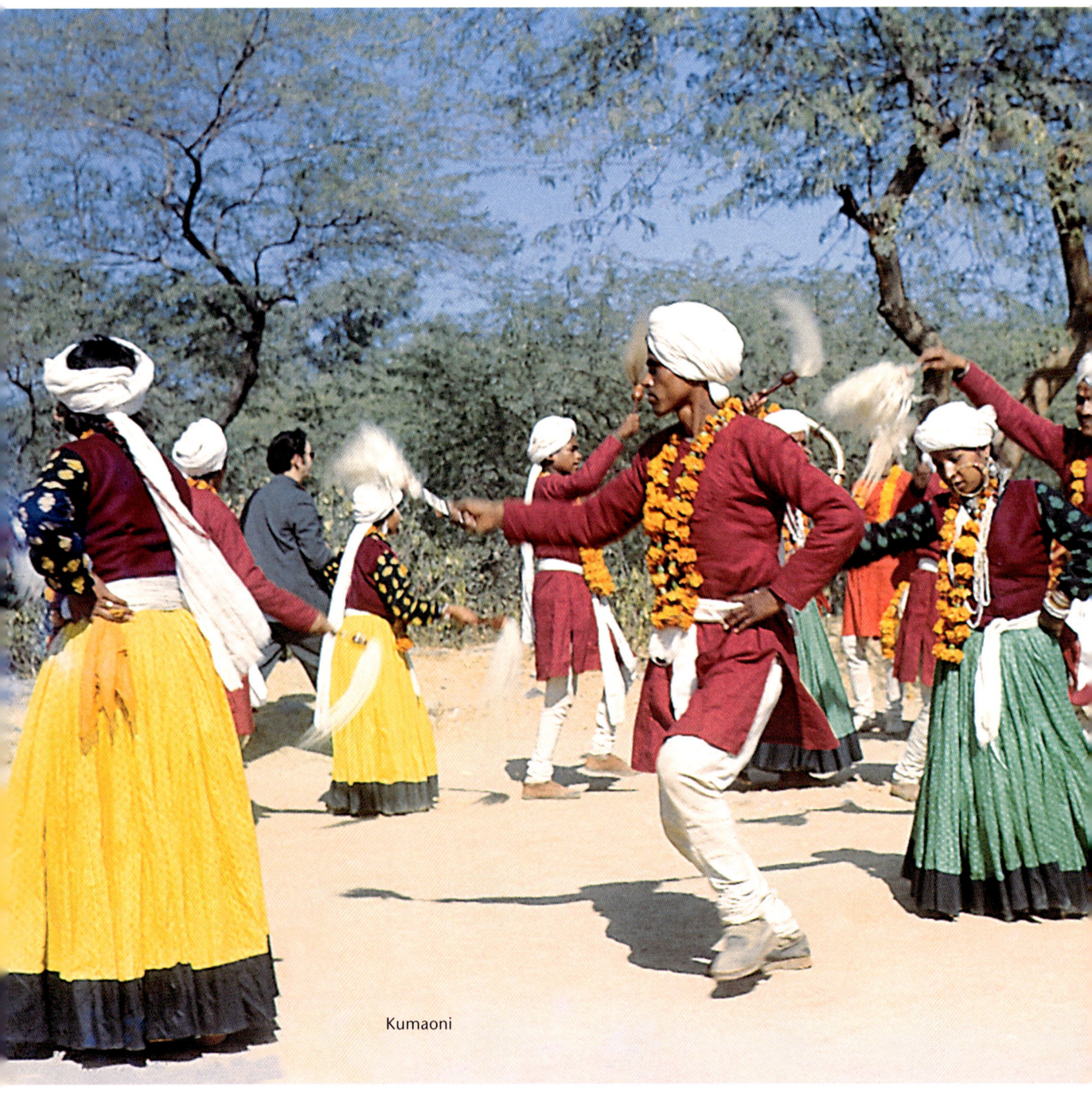

Kumaoni

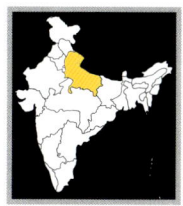

f i v e

UTTAR PRADESH

Welcome to the Indo-Gangetic plain – to the state where quiet flows the Ganga, the mighty river that has been associated with India from time immemorial. The land of Uttar Pradesh, watered not only by the Ganga, but many other rivers as well, is sumptuously fertile. The Garhwal mountains lie to the north of this state. In its heartland, the Gangetic plains, there are several old cities buzzing with industrial activity, and also umpteen villages that dance to a completely different beat. The people of Uttar Pradesh are gregarious and easy-going and they love light-hearted fun. Their customs reflect the joy of living life to the fullest. Life, for them, is a series of festivities – births, weddings, family reunions – and all occasions call for spontaneous celebrations marked by plenty of singing and dancing.

Kedar is a dance form of Kedarnath and Badrinath, two shrines in the rugged terrain of northern Uttar Pradesh that are dedicated to Shiva and Vishnu. These temples have been the source of a good deal of folklore and tradition. Kedar dancers carry *chamars* (sacred whisks or fans) that are swished back and forth all through the performance.

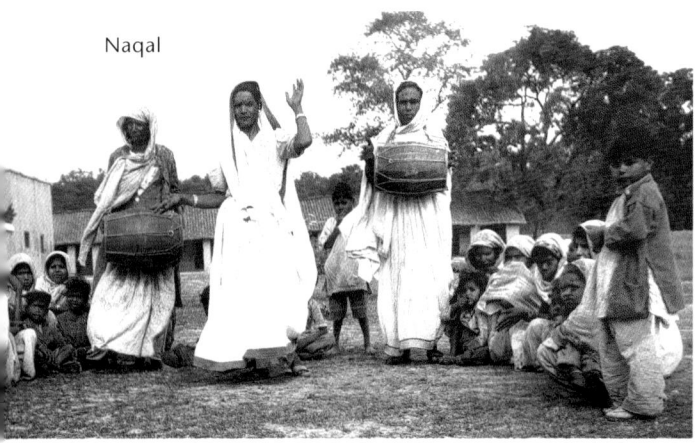

Naqal

Naqal means imitation, and this lively dance-drama form borrows freely from various traditions of this region to act out popular tales. A contemporary twist is given to the tales by incorporating a spicy and uproarious commentary on the activities in high society. Thus the rural audience is both entertained as well as informed.

Sakhia is danced by the Thoras, an agricultural tribe. It is performed mostly on festivals like Holi and Dusshera. The women carry small cymbals in hand and the men accompany them on the drums and dance along sportingly.

The hill people of Kumaon and Garhwal need no special occasion to break into a dance. They dance naturally, without any particular reason. Their music is sweet and lilting and the setting, beautiful. Sometimes their dance is a kind of rejoicing while at others, it is inspired by the simple need to propitiate Mother Nature.

The **Karma** dance originated in the Mirzapur region and is connected to a fertility ritual. A new, green branch of a tree, symbolising abundance, is offered to the Karma God. The village priest presides over the ritual. The villagers dance, the priest joins in and often falls into a trance while dancing.

Raas-Leela is a popular dance-drama of the Braj region. Pre-pubescent boys dress up as *gopis* (young village girls who, in Indian mythology, were enamoured of Krishna), and swarm and dance around the lead dancer playing Krishna. They enact several well-known episodes from Krishna's early life as a flute-playing charmer. This evergreen group dance is staged throughout the year, and especially at Janmashtami, the occasion observed as Krishna's birthday.

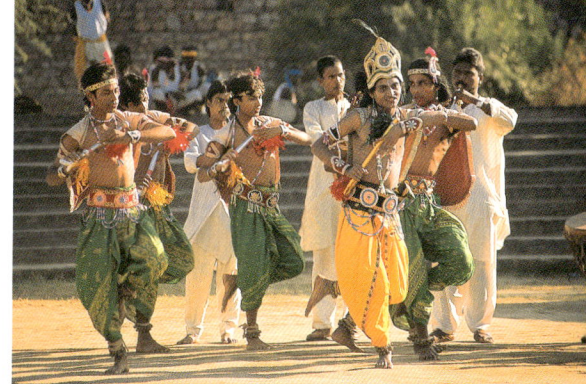

Raas-Leela

The folk dance known as **Saina** requires a degree of skill and practice. The performers deftly manipulate a metal plate, flinging it into the air and catching it by turns, dancing all the while. This style belongs to the Jaunsar-Bawar region, and both men and women participate in the dance.

Chholiya, a dance of Kumaon, is performed at wedding ceremonies, and also when the marriage procession wends its way through the lanes. Generally, only male dancers perform this dance. Armed with swords and shields, they show off their muscular strength through energetic movements.

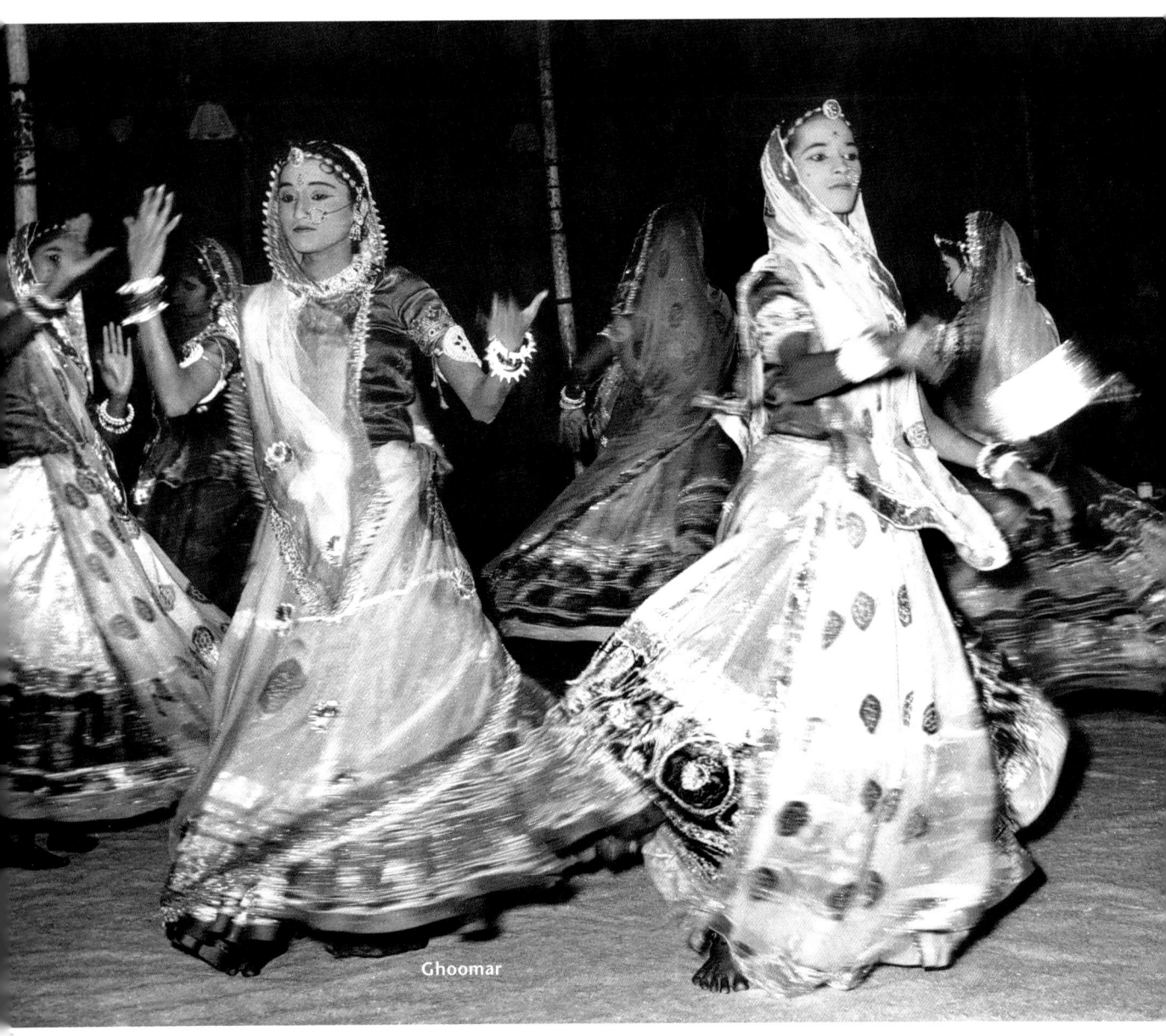

Ghoomar

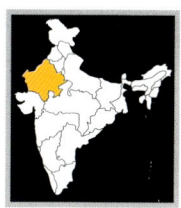

s i x

Rajasthan

A state that conjures up the image of parched earth, bleak landscape, and no relief. But the people and their colourful costume break the monotony of the desert landscape and make it come alive. This Indian state represents the triumph of human life against great odds, daily trials and tribulations. The Rajasthanis are a proud race, people who are prepared (as history tells) for every sacrifice to guard their land and their honour. The many forts, palaces, and *havelis* (old, sprawling houses built for the aristocrats) of Rajasthan are pointers to their quintessential character, the way they adapted to their environment, grappled with marauding invaders, and yet developed and protected a distinctive culture. Their dances, too, reflect their bravery.

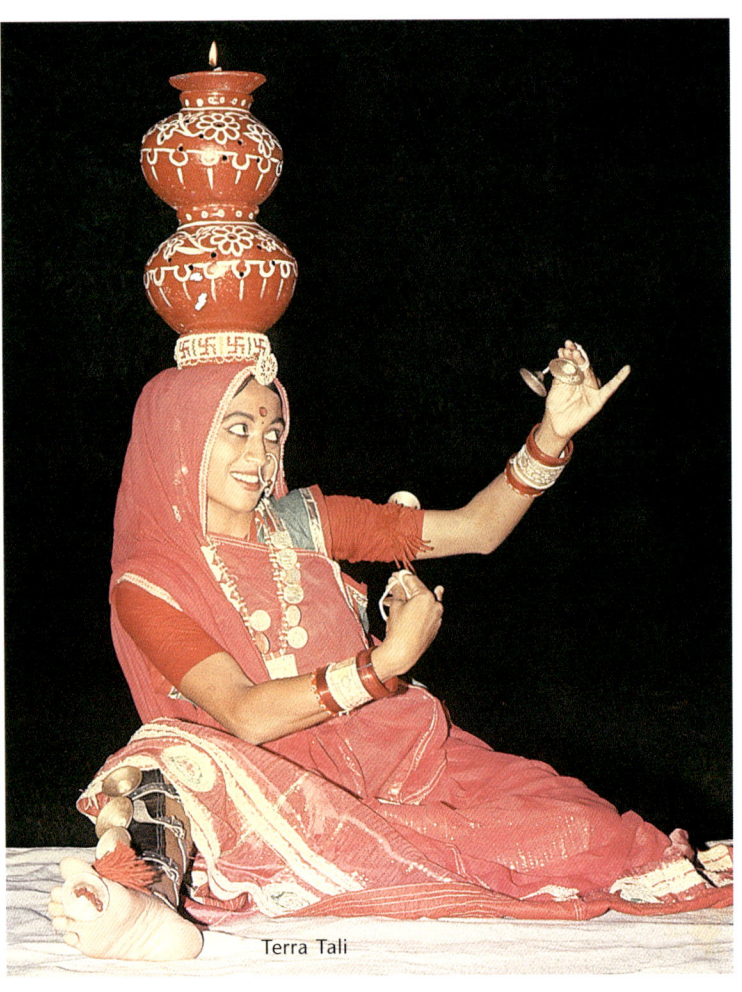

Terra Tali

Terra Tali is the most popular and famous of Rajasthani folk dance forms. In this, two or more women sit and sway and strike cymbals tied to different parts of their limbs. They maintain a fast rhythm and try several spontaneous combinations of limb movement. Every performer wears a veil pulled down over most of her face. They clench a dagger between the teeth and balance a small earthen pitcher upon the head. Thus the dancers expertly undertake many feats in one go, making it all look very simple.

Ghoomar is another well-known dance form of Rajasthan. The dancers, all women, wear voluminous long skirts that fan out as they twirl. A lot of clapping accompanies the proceedings. The billowing skirts look like clouds floating in the sky, a captivating sight for sore eyes in this desert land.

In **Khayal** dance style, local legends and tales of valour dear to a Rajput's heart are depicted through music and dance. Stylised acting and singing, by men only, form a core part of this rendition.

The Kanjar tribals perform the **Dhakar** as a kind of thanksgiving rite. Both men and women carry axes and shields and perform this martial dance. Some heavy drumming adds to its overall effect.

Kacchi Ghori is the dummy-horse dance of Rajasthan, a tradition popular in other parts of India too, like Tamil Nadu, Kashmir, and Bengal. A man stands in a dummy horse so

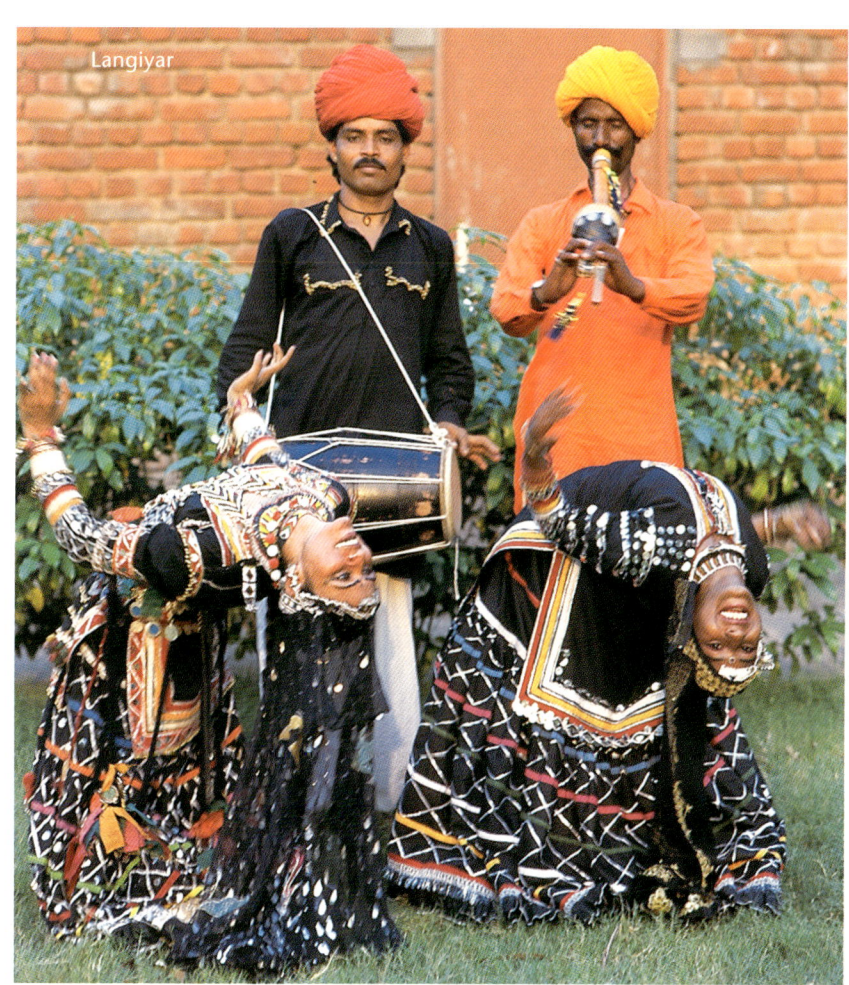

Langiyar

that only his torso and head are visible, and he dances around, as though riding a galloping horse, singing of the might of kings and heroes.

The **Panihari** dance by women is an exhibition of intricate movement and great balancing skills. The women perform this slow dance while balancing several water-filled pots on their heads. Obviously, it requires finely honed skills to keep moving in a pattern and yet keep the pots balanced on the head so that not even a drop of water is spilt.

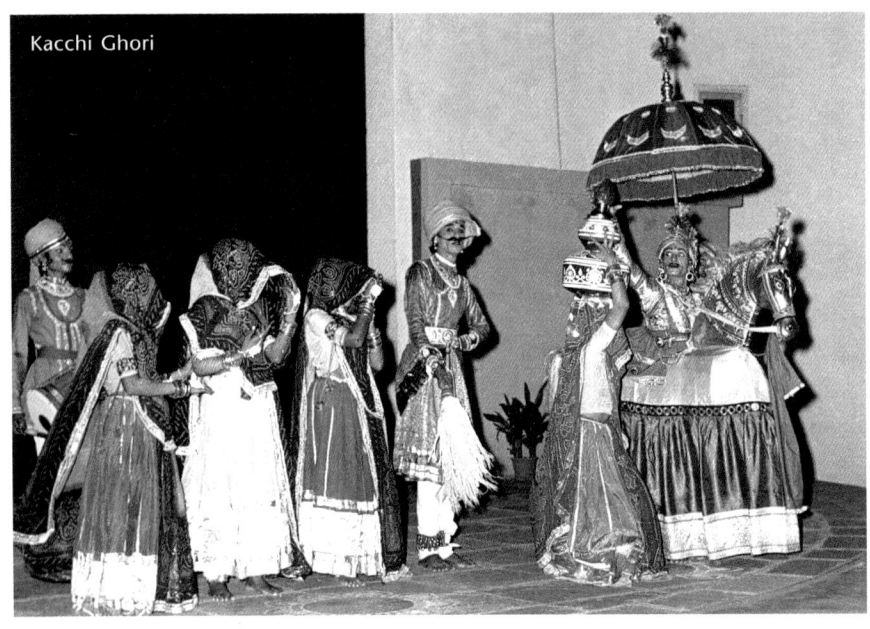

Kacchi Ghori

Gauri is performed by the Bheel tribe of Rajasthan. Performed during the rains, and only during daytime, this style is based on the theme of Shiva as Bhairav who destroys Bhasmasura, the nihilist demon. Often masks are used to dramatise the story.

Charwas or **Chari** is danced by *malis*, who are flower-gatherers or gardeners. In this daring dance, the performers balance upon their heads several pots that have lit *diyas* (tiny earthen bowls with oil and wicks) in them. The little tongues of flame do a dance of their own, forming a fascinating pattern, while the dancers swirl and whirl.

Yet another tribute to Rajasthani daredevilry, **Bhavai** is a dance that displays acrobatic feats. Again, the dancers balance several pots on their head, but this time their movement is not sedate and slow. Instead, they actually jump without disturbing their pots. Both men and women perform the *Bhavai*. This dance is being increasingly staged in cities these days for the benefit of tourists.

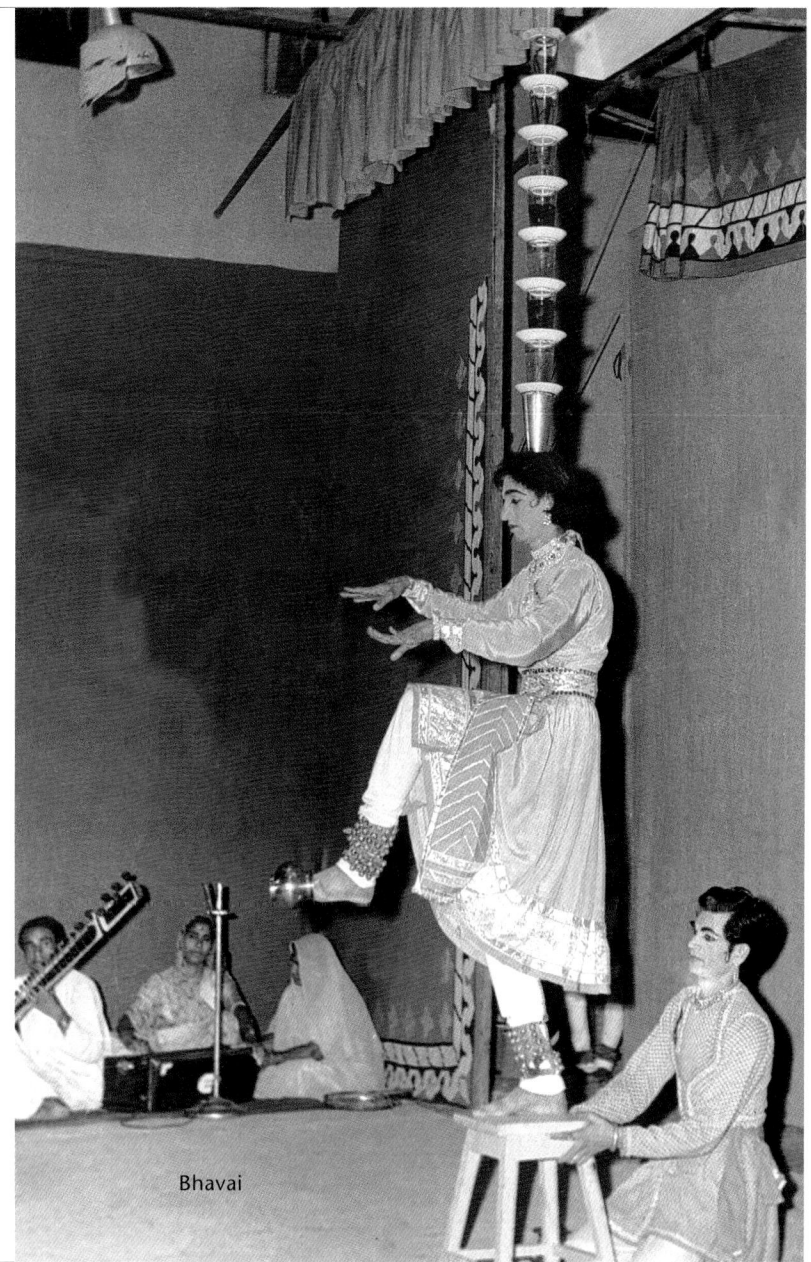

Bhavai

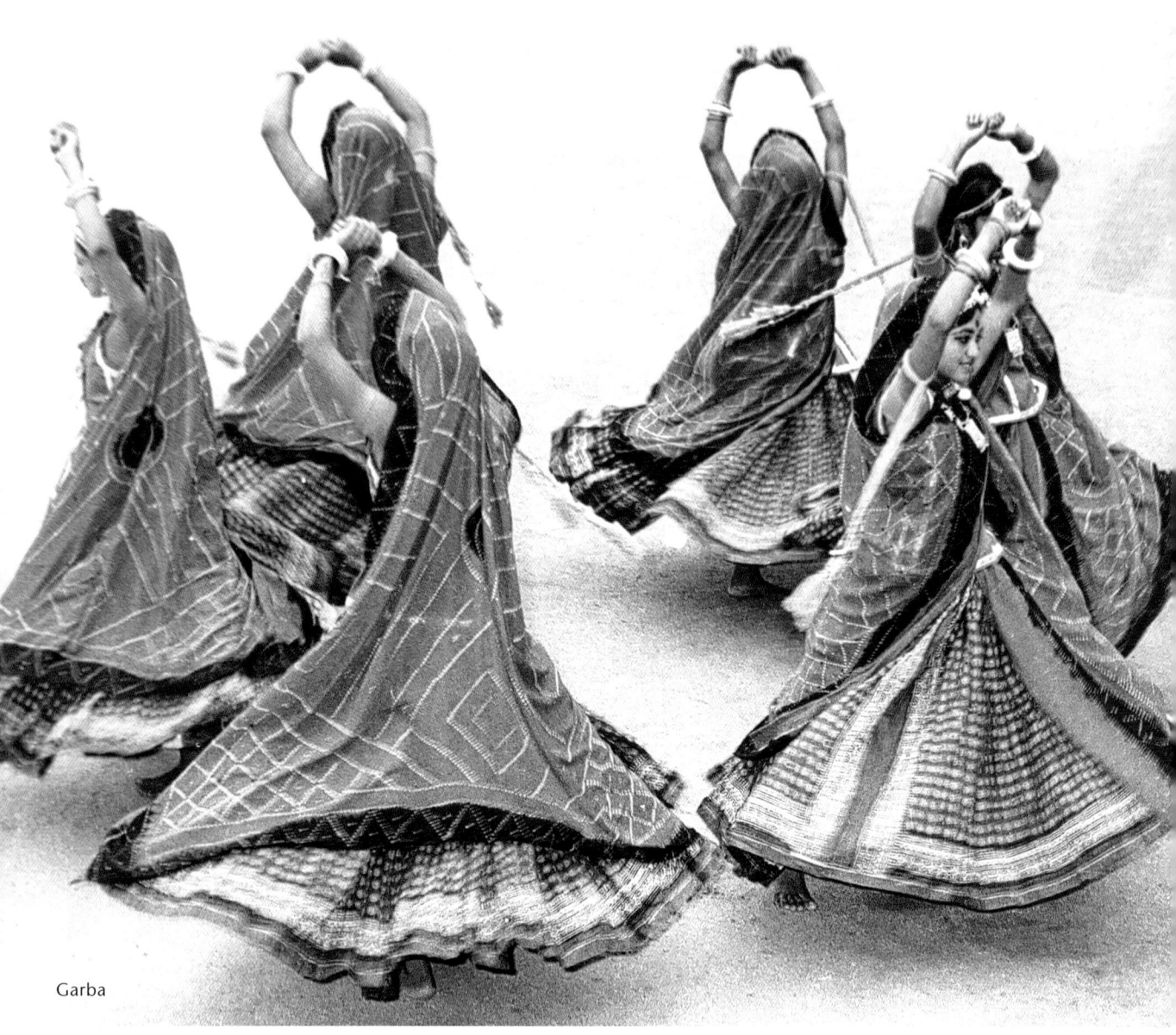
Garba

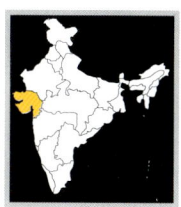

s e v e n

GUJARAT

Gujarat is a wealthy western state of India, where people take pleasure as seriously as they do tenacious work and industry. It holds the rare distinction of being just about the only place in twenty-first century India where the urban-rural divide blurs when it comes to celebrating folk forms.

Garba is the most popular and frequently performed folk dance of Gujarat. It is a dance in which large groups participate. It takes place during Navratri, nine nights in autumn when Goddess Amba/Durga/Shakti/Parvati is communally worshipped in India. Women clap and move to a simple beat, balancing on their heads earthen pots that contain burning lamps. When men perform it, the style is called **Garbi**. While traditionally the Garba is danced at night during Navratri, the dance is nowadays performed on just about any

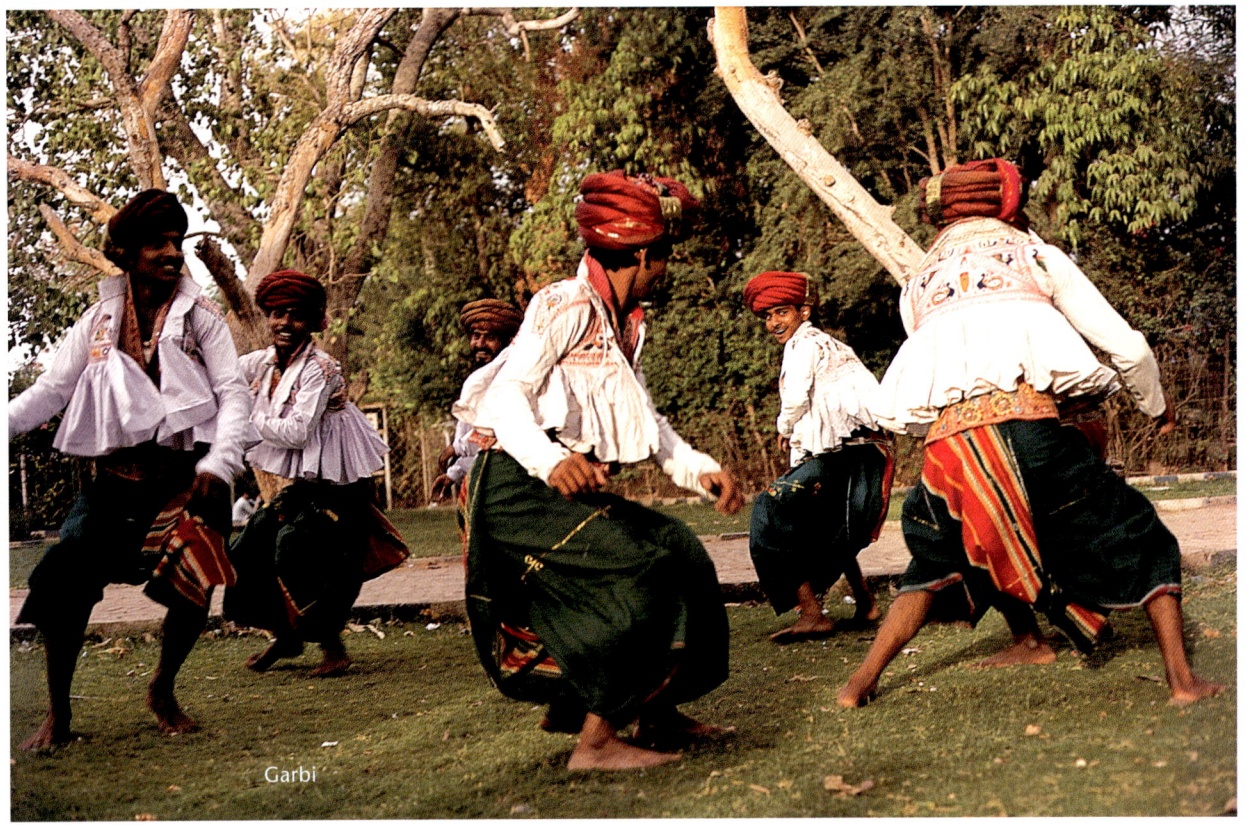

Garbi

occasion. Usually, loud rhythmic clapping keeps the brisk tempo, but sometimes even mere snapping of fingers is enough. Occasionally, instead of pots, the women balance winnowing trays on their heads.

Ras, which celebrates the love-dance of the *gopis* with Radha and Krishna, is also performed during Navratri. Both men and women take part, forming circular patterns and weaving different choreographic designs. When the dancers also carry sticks, which they clank stylishly while sweeping past each other, the form is dubbed as Dandiya Ras. Dandiya is much in vogue, even in city settings, during large community get-togethers.

Bhavai is a form of folk drama, which is an extremely popular form of entertainment. A series of cameo presentations, called *veshas*, take place where the comical or farcical element is predominant. Dancing is an integral part of the

Dandiya

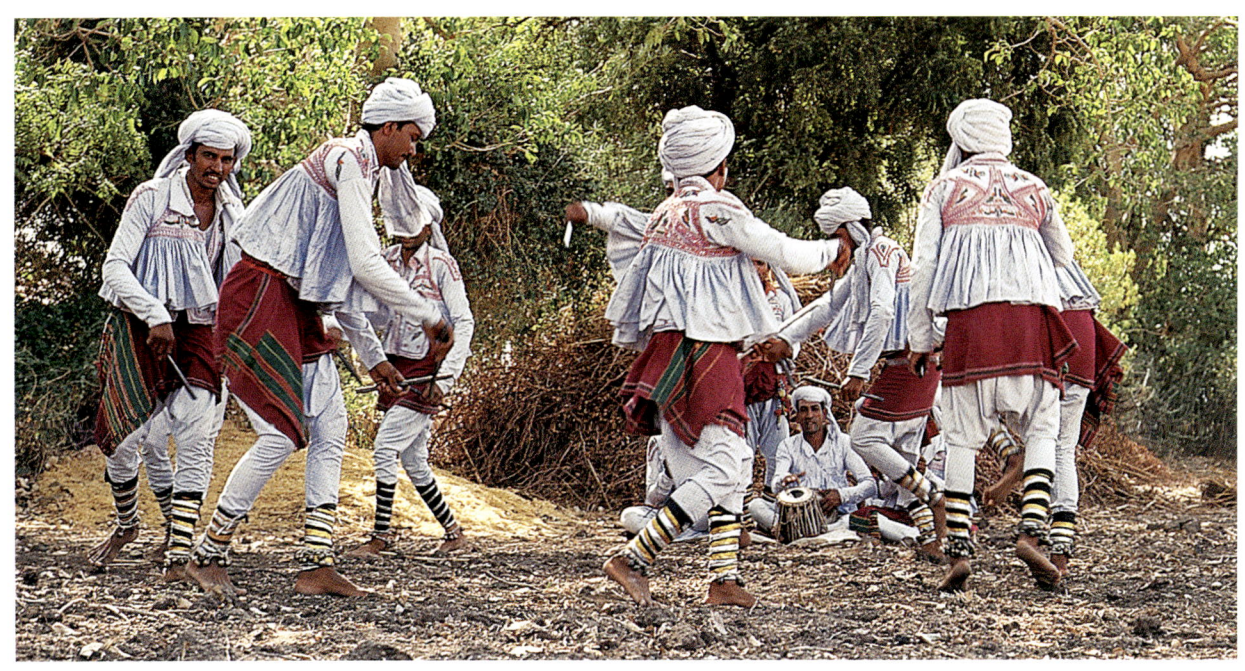

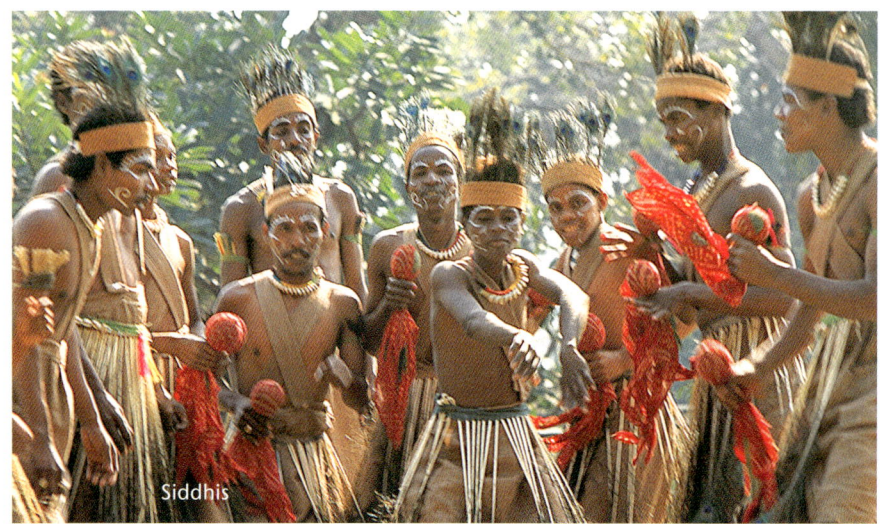
Siddhis

proceedings. The performers are mostly men, who are adept at acrobatic antics as well as jugglery.

Tippani is among a handful of folk dances in India that actually serve some practical function even while entertaining. In this particular case, the dancers, who are basically workers at a construction site, beat the floor with wooden mallets. Thus, they enliven a tedious chore by singing and moving on the job! The mallets, hitting the floor at regular intervals, produce a 'tip-tip' sound, hence the name of the dance.

Dangi dance calls for agile men and women who can form human pyramids by climbing on each other's shoulders in tiers. They move in circles and other geometrical patterns to present a visually exciting and finely synchronised show. Much jumping and bending takes place, emphasising the athletic quality of this group dance. It is an artistic, down-to-earth version of an aerobics routine, but of course, needing superior levels of fitness and flexibility.

The **Bheels** of Gujarat, who live in an area bordering Rajasthan, have an eponymous dance that is performed with bows and arrows. Since hunting and food gathering is a part and parcel of their daily routine, they weld it with dance. Often a mock hunt is arranged and the dancers take pride in showing off their skills. The **Siddhis** hail from the African stock and are an indigenous tribe of Gujarat. Their dance is full of vigorous acrobatic movements.

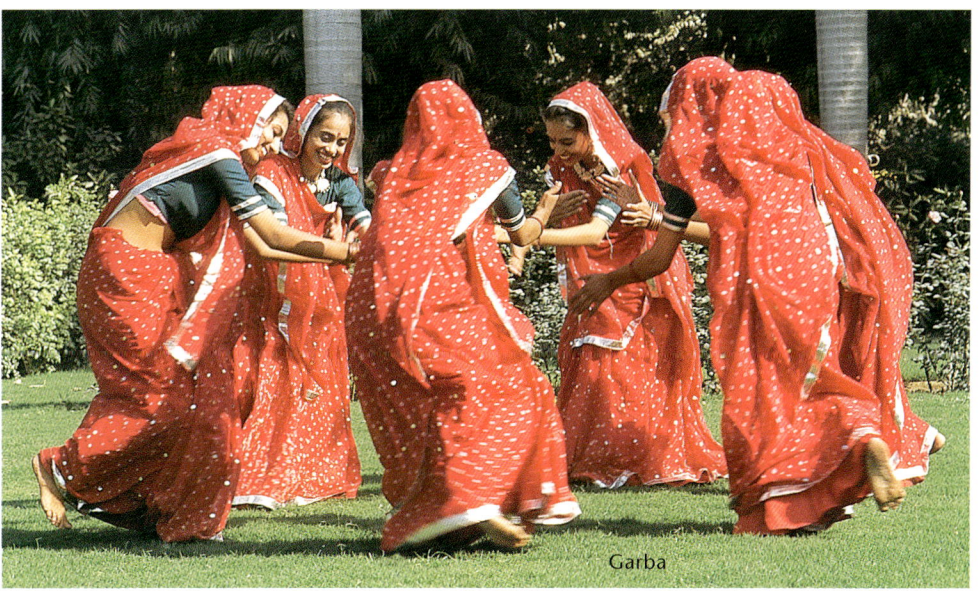

Garba

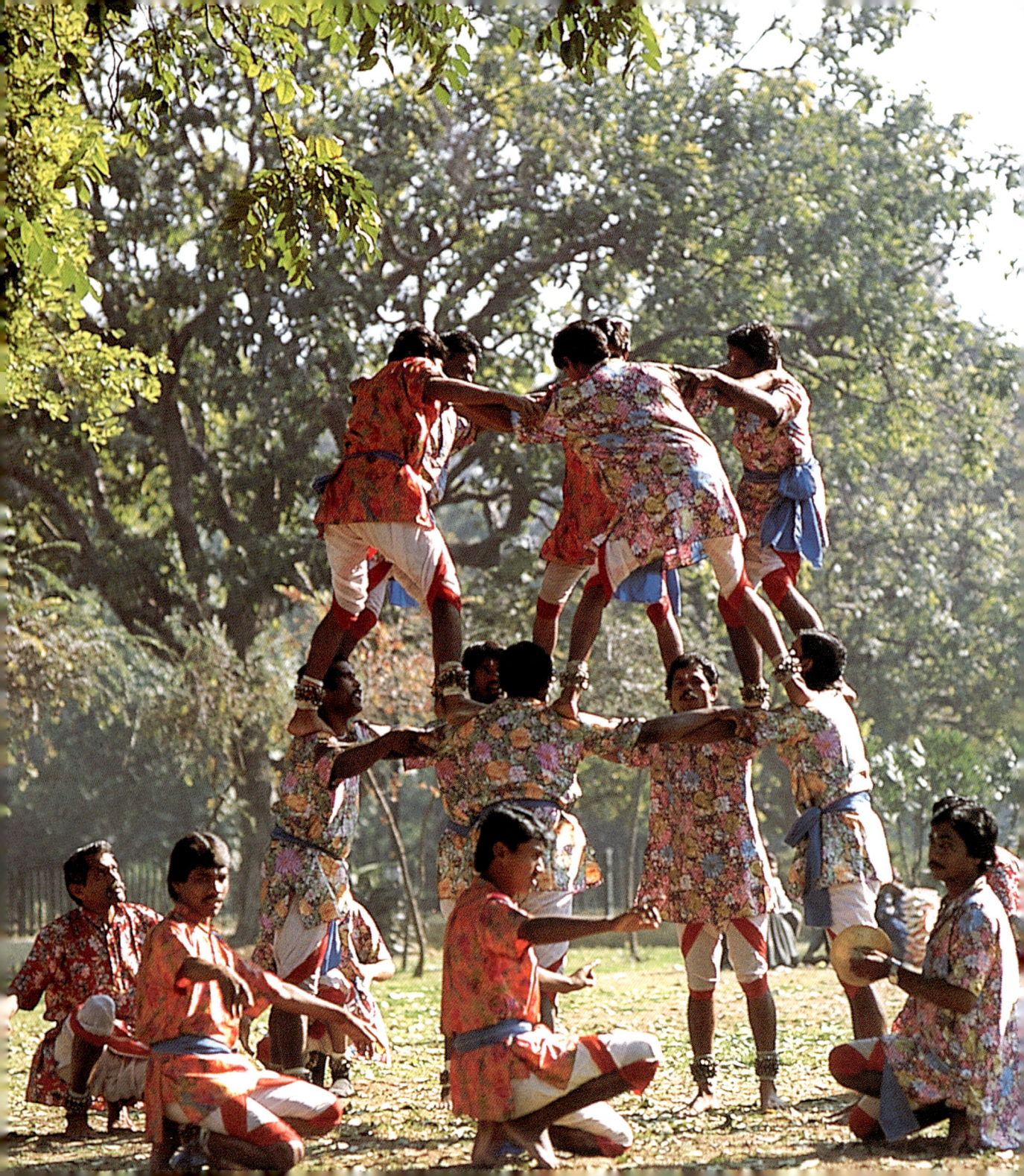

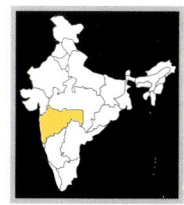

e i g h t

MAHARASHTRA

irded by the Arabian Sea on one side and by forests on the other, this cotton-rich state has a wide variety of sparkling dance forms. The state is rich in art and culture, commerce and history, and the Maharashtrians fastidiously retain the purity of all their cultural traditions, including the varied folk dances.

Bohada is a ritual dance of the Kokna and Warli tribals who live in the north-western part of the state. Generally performed in April-May, this form of dance involves one and all. Masked dancers propitiate the presiding deities of their households. Men wear huge, scary masks to ward off evil spirits, and flock down the lanes, as if driving these spirits away from their village.

opp.
Tarpha Nach

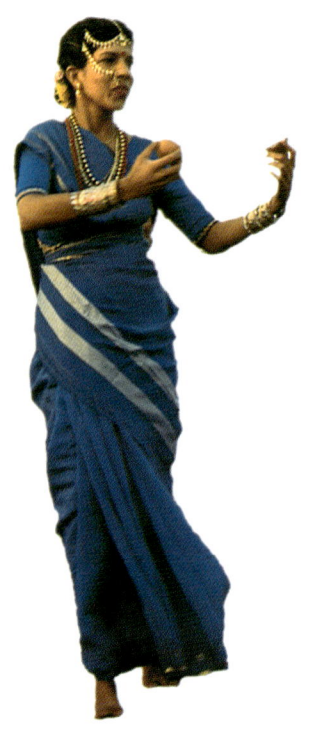

Koli

Jagran is a dance-drama performed in honour of Khandoba, a deity, and his consort, Mhalsa. It is enacted by people called *vaghya*s and *murali*s, who are dedicated at birth to the service of Khandoba. These performers are highly revered because of their special status and through their dance they bring alive the glorious legends surrounding Khandoba.

Dashavtar is a dance of the Konkan region, the coastal stretch of Maharashtra that is rich in myths and legends. Dashavtar is a part of temple festivities and is performed only by men. The presentation is generally clearly split into dance and drama. The opening sequence usually eulogises Ganesha, Saraswati, or Vishnu and involves a great deal of dancing. The performance involves the dramatic appearance and stellar turns of celestial beings.

Tarpha Nach is the dance of the tribals of Kokna. They fashion a wind instrument out of dried gourd, which is beautifully decorated. They dance in a group, form a series of pyramidal patterns and use sticks and also a pole to dance around.

The **Koli** fisherfolk have several attractive and colourful dances to celebrate virtually any joyous occasion, for instance, the fun spring festival of Holi.

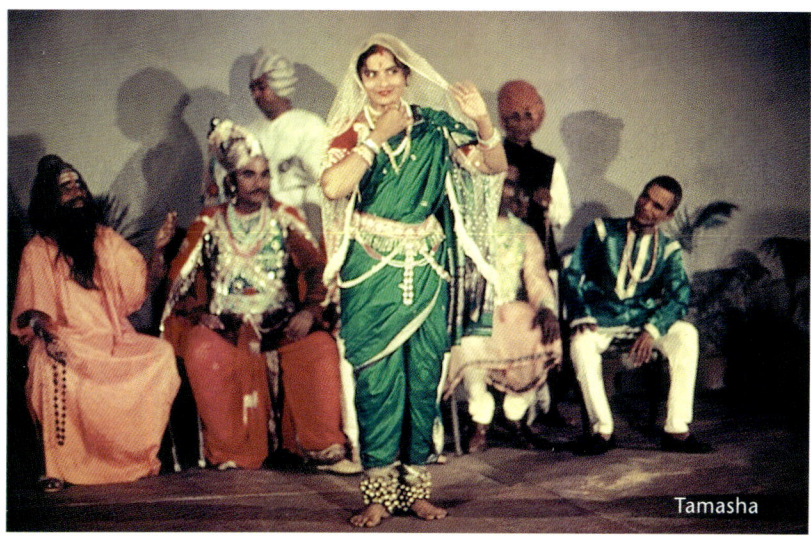

Tamasha

Tamasha is the extremely popular dance-drama that represents the folk aspirations and culture of Maharashtra. The theme may be drawn from either mythology or contemporary society. Only women perform it. The dance part of it is called **Lavani,** which is deliberately titillating and a telling pointer to popular tastes.

Lavani can also be performed by itself. It has a liberal dose of suggestive sexual flourishes and much pelvic thrusting. These elements have been readily absorbed into the dance vocabulary of the region, of which the Mumbai film industry is an integral part.

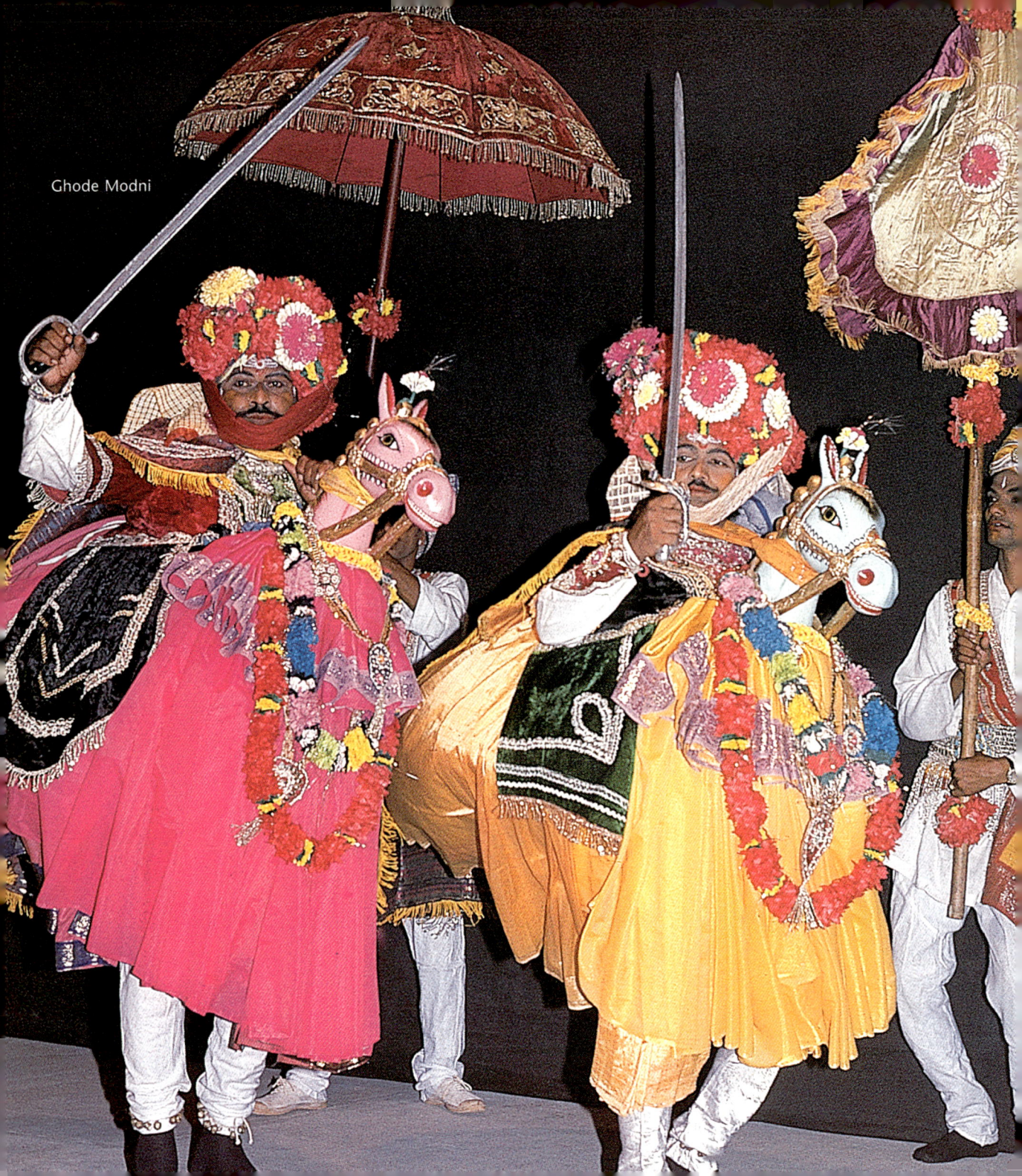

Ghode Modni

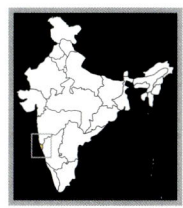

n i n e

GOA

The grand **Carnival** of Goa is an annual event during which people (including visitors from all over the world) dance and boogie with gay abandon and – for three days – give themselves up to unabashed merrymaking. Huge processions weave through the streets of Goa. Human puppets, singers, jugglers, and dancers take part in these processions.

Dashavtar and **Ghode Modni** are two popular dance forms of Goa, borrowed from the neighbouring state of Maharashtra and danced in much the same way.

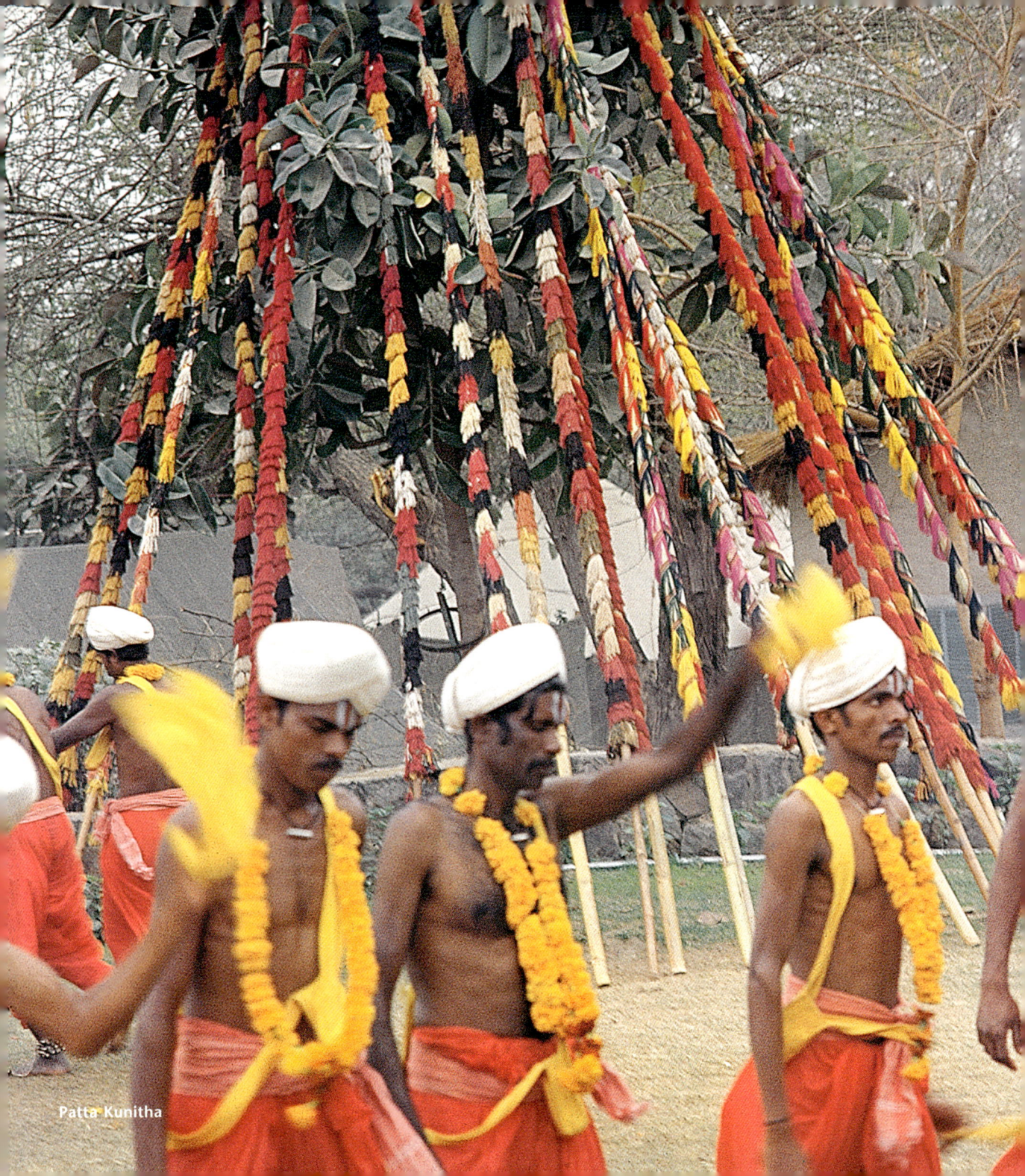

Patta Kunitha

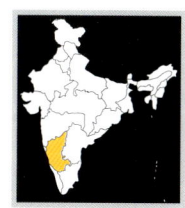

t e n

KARNATAKA

Coffee estates, white sand beaches, and gentle people – welcome you to Karnataka. This southern state of India has many folk dance forms, as the populace is largely pastoral. Enjoying a good climate the year round, the Kannadiga generally do not have to struggle with the vagaries of nature. In fact, they take joy in the cycle of seasons.

Kamsale is a dance performed by men wielding cymbals. It was originally a dance with religious connotations but has increasingly been adapted for secular, celebratory functions. Men wear gaudy costumes and dance either solo or in groups. The foot-tapping music plays around with rhythm while maintaining a particular beat.

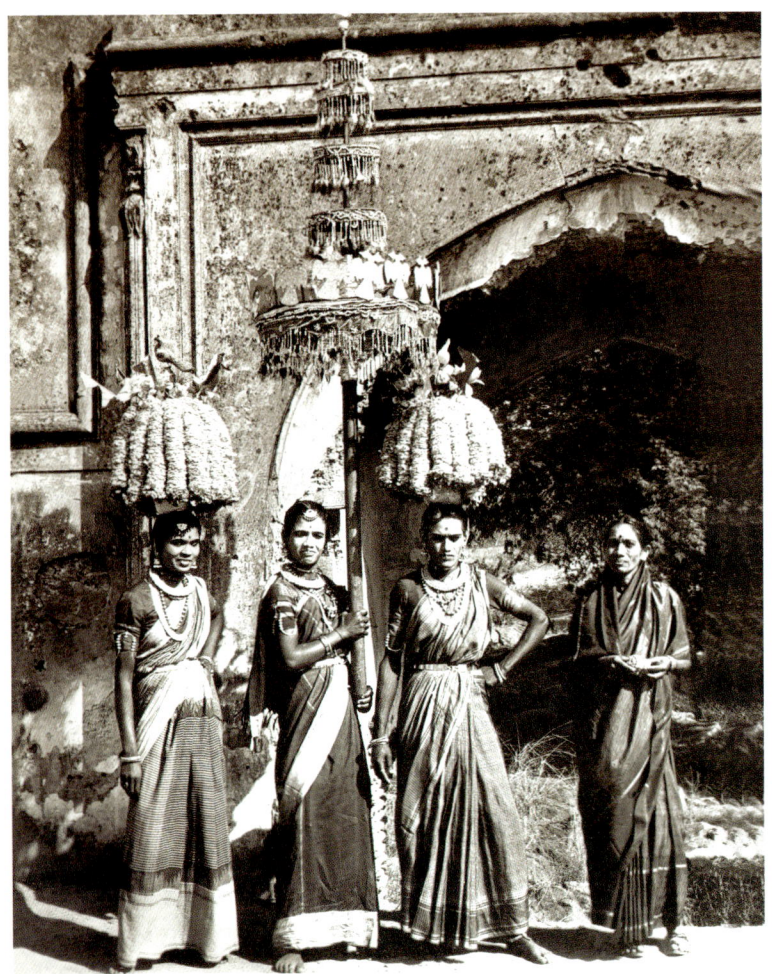

Dollu Kunitha is the boisterous drum dance of Karnataka, which is highly popular. Large drums adorned with traditional motifs are used. The dancers, usually an all-male team, undertake stunning acrobatic feats. The drums have a mesmerising effect as they vary the tempo, and the flurry of limbs as the lithe dancers leap and somersault, give an endearing impression of brimming energy and confident youthfulness.

Patta Kunitha is a variation of the Dollu Kunitha. In this dance, instead of drums, bamboo poles decorated with ribbons are used. These poles are crowned with silver and brass bells that tinkle and jangle when the dancers perform.

Bhootam is a dance of coastal Karnataka. It has animistic elements and is ritualistic in form. Only male dancers perform it. The extensive preparations before the actual performance and the fact that coconut and palmyra leaves are used for making the dance costumes, call for patience and perseverance. The presentation takes place in

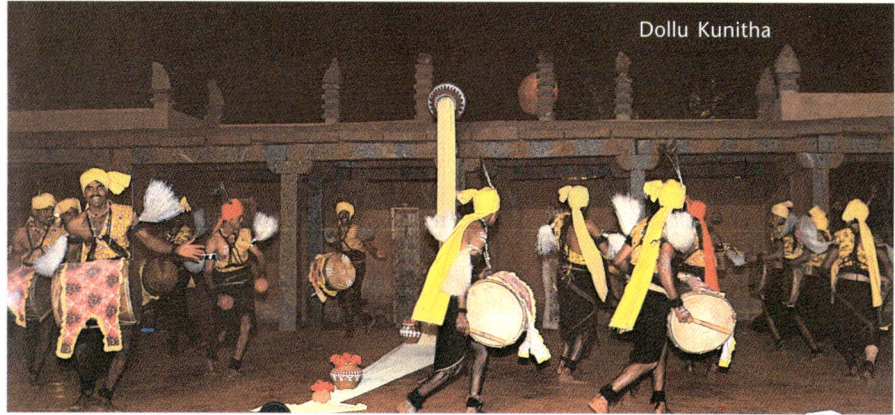

Dollu Kunitha

front of idols of the village deities, usually carved out of wood and painted in bold colours.

The **Kola** dances are an extension of Bhootam, but in this form, the dancers actually identify themselves with particular deities. It is common especially in Makkekatte, a place which is considered the epicenter of this tradition. Over 200 woodcarvings of various deities abound in this village.

Balakattu belongs to Coorg, a beautiful hilly region with miles of coffee and cashew plantations. The Coorgs are a handsome and courageous people. They enjoy life and have countless occasions and

opp.
Chombu Karaga

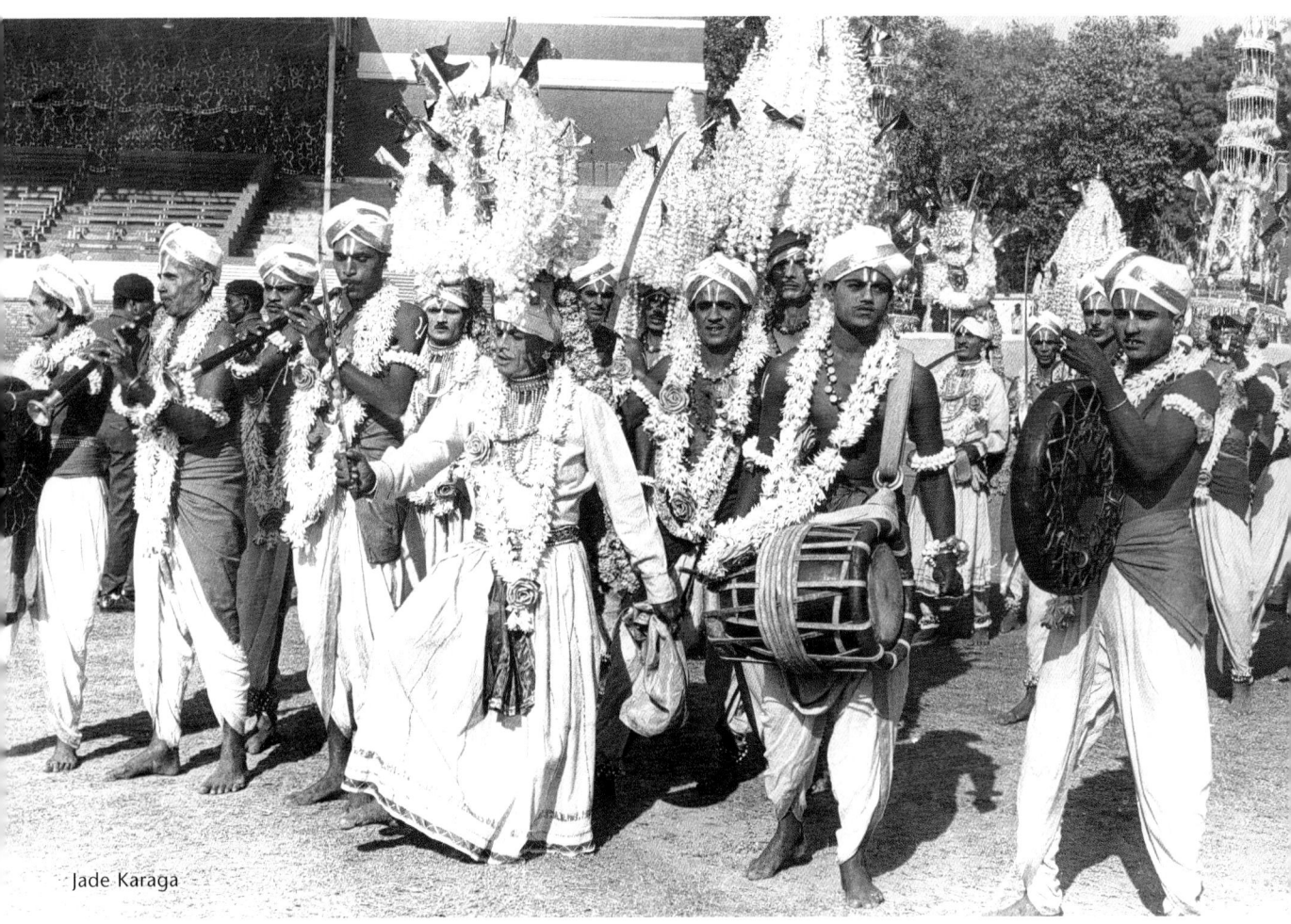

Jade Karaga

abundant resources for indulgence. Their best, however, is reserved for weddings when, attired in their traditional silken outfits, they dance the vigorous Balakattu.

Pooja Kunitha is a sacred dance performed only by the priests of the local temples. It involves balancing a large wooden idol on the head and dancing to the accompaniment of a drum.

Karaga is a solo ritual dance. It permits lots of different combinations, so there is some scope for originality and improvisation. The Jade Karaga is the most awesome of the usual forms, in which the performer is burdened with a massive head–dress comprising a heavy cluster of flowers. As the dancer goes through his steps, the flowers and garlands twine and wave about, forming picturesque patterns. Soon the place is strewn and fragrant with flowers that have fallen off from the head–dress. This dance is essentially a solo style but is often performed in pairs, too. During religious festivals, the form occasionally dovetails into the **Pooja Kunitha**.

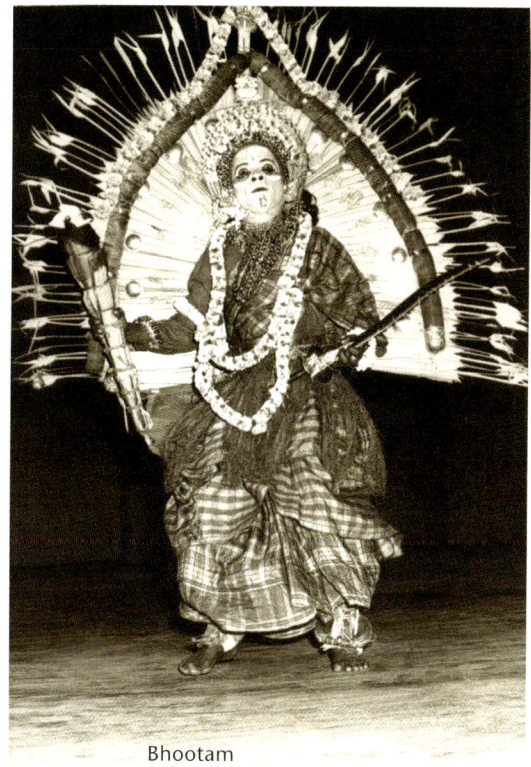
Bhootam

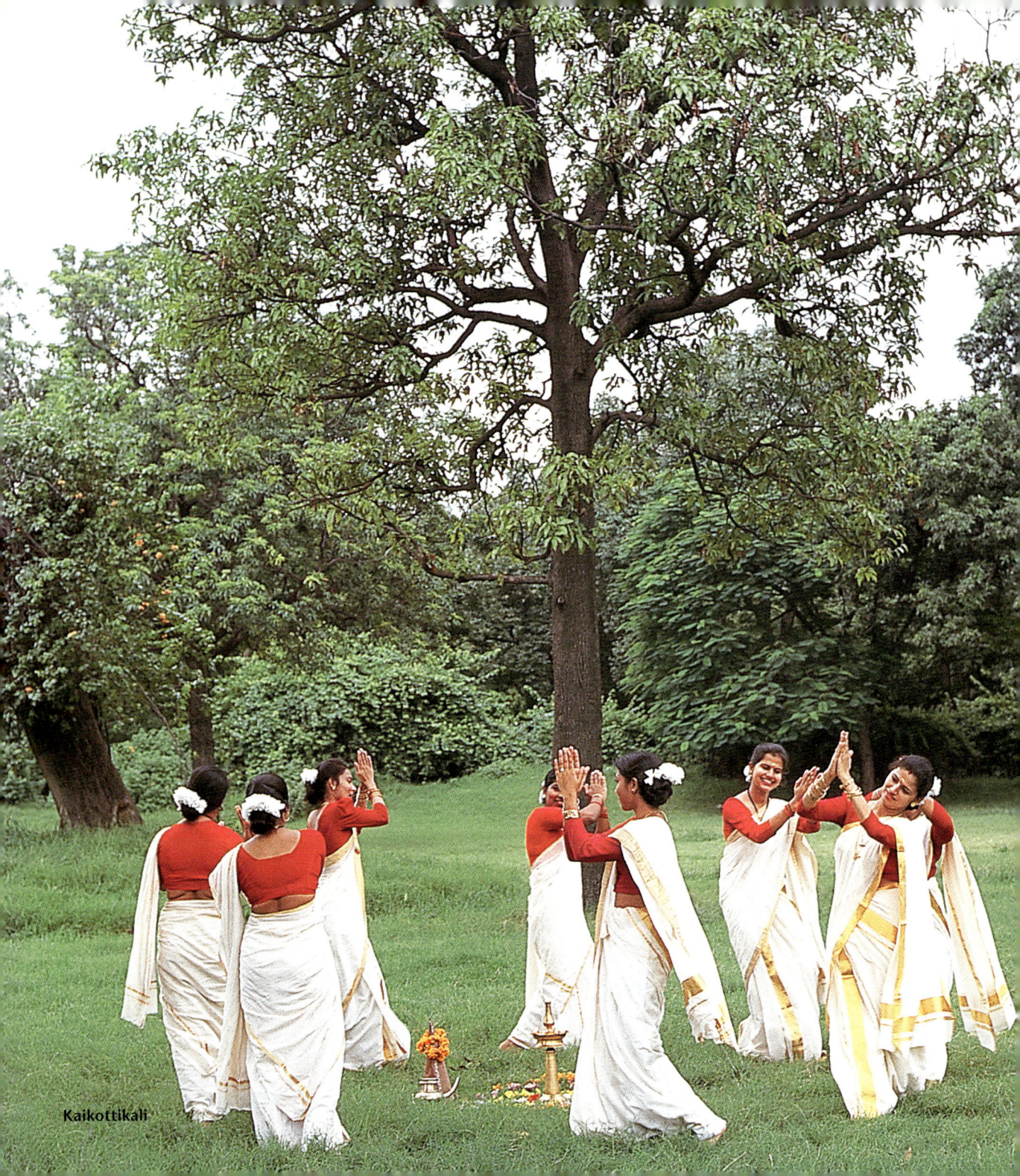

Kaikottikali

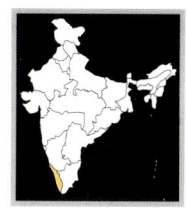

e l e v e n

KERALA

The lush green scenery of Kerala is a sight for the gods themselves! Indeed, the gods here are propitiated in various ways, of which folk dance forms are the most extensive. Paddy and coconut fields provide the natural theatre for the people to stage their dances. In addition to worshipping numerous traditional deities, the dances also enjoin people to express joy at nature's abundant gifts.

Kaikottikali is an important dance of the women of Kerala. It is performed at Onam, Kerala's most important festival. Legend has it that Onam originated when King Bahubali returned to his land after a prolonged absence. His subjects welcomed him back with pomp and ceremony. The return of a benevolent and puissant king signifies the return of prosperity and peace to a land. That is what Onam

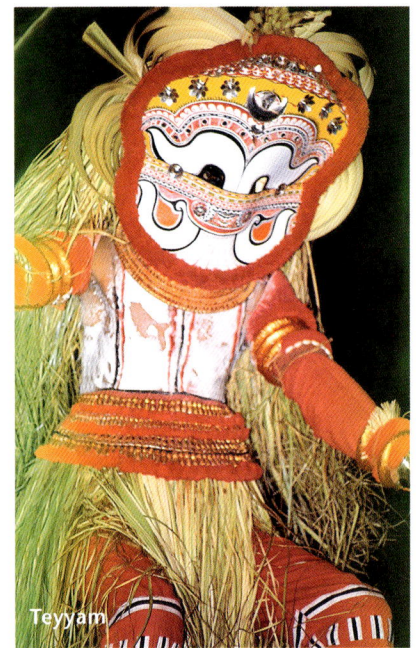
Teyyam

represents, which is why legends trace the very birth of Kerala to King Bahubali's return and to the first Onam. In the Kaikottikali dance style, women place a lamp at the centre of an artistically decorated performance area and then sing and dance around it, moving with simple but graceful steps.

Velakali is performed by the Nair community during festivities at the Padmanabhaswamy temple in Thiruvananthapuram, the state capital. The male dancers, costumed in combat gear, demonstrate the martial character of the people of Kerala by carrying swords and shields.

Thiruvadirakali is danced by women on the occasion of the Thiruvadira festival, on moonlit nights. Soft crooning and much clapping add to the lyricism of the atmosphere. The dance form resembles the Kaikottikali but in this form only adult women take part.

Kolam Thullal is a ritual dance of the so-called lower castes, performed by men. The dance honours Kali or Bhadrakali, the reigning goddess of Kerala. Huge masks and headdresses are used and, after the performance, discarded by way of ritual completion.

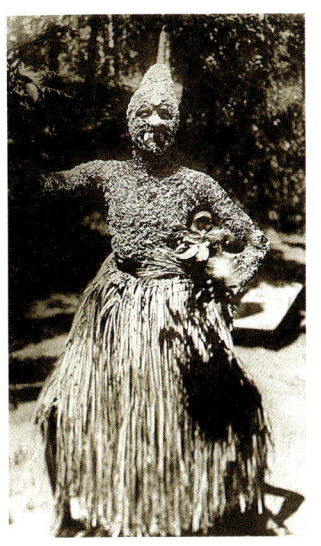

Mudiyettu is the earliest form of ritual theatre in Kerala. It preceded Koodiyattam, Krishnattam and Ramnattam. In this, the demon Darika is vanquished by Bhadrakali. The costume is awesome and hideous enough to frighten the village audience that assembles at night when it is usually performed.

Teyyam is a major ritual dance performed annually in north Kerala. It is danced in honour of Goddess Bhagwati and her associates, who number over fifty. Painted faces, gorgeous costumes, and gleaming jewellery make the Teyyam a visual feast.

left: Nenaveli

Nenaveli is performed to ward off the dreaded smallpox. The dancers smear their bodies with lime and unhusked rice to convey an impression of the fatal disease.

Kalaripayattu is chief martial form of Kerala, used for combat and originally patronised by the Zamorin rulers. The form is known by its pithy name — Kalari — and has become an important sport too.

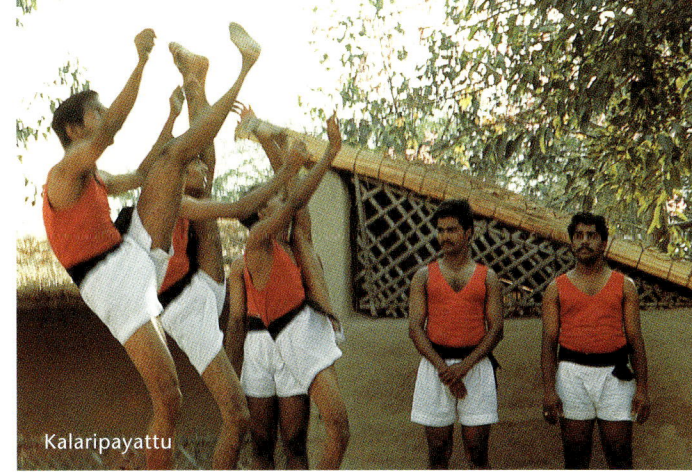

Kalaripayattu

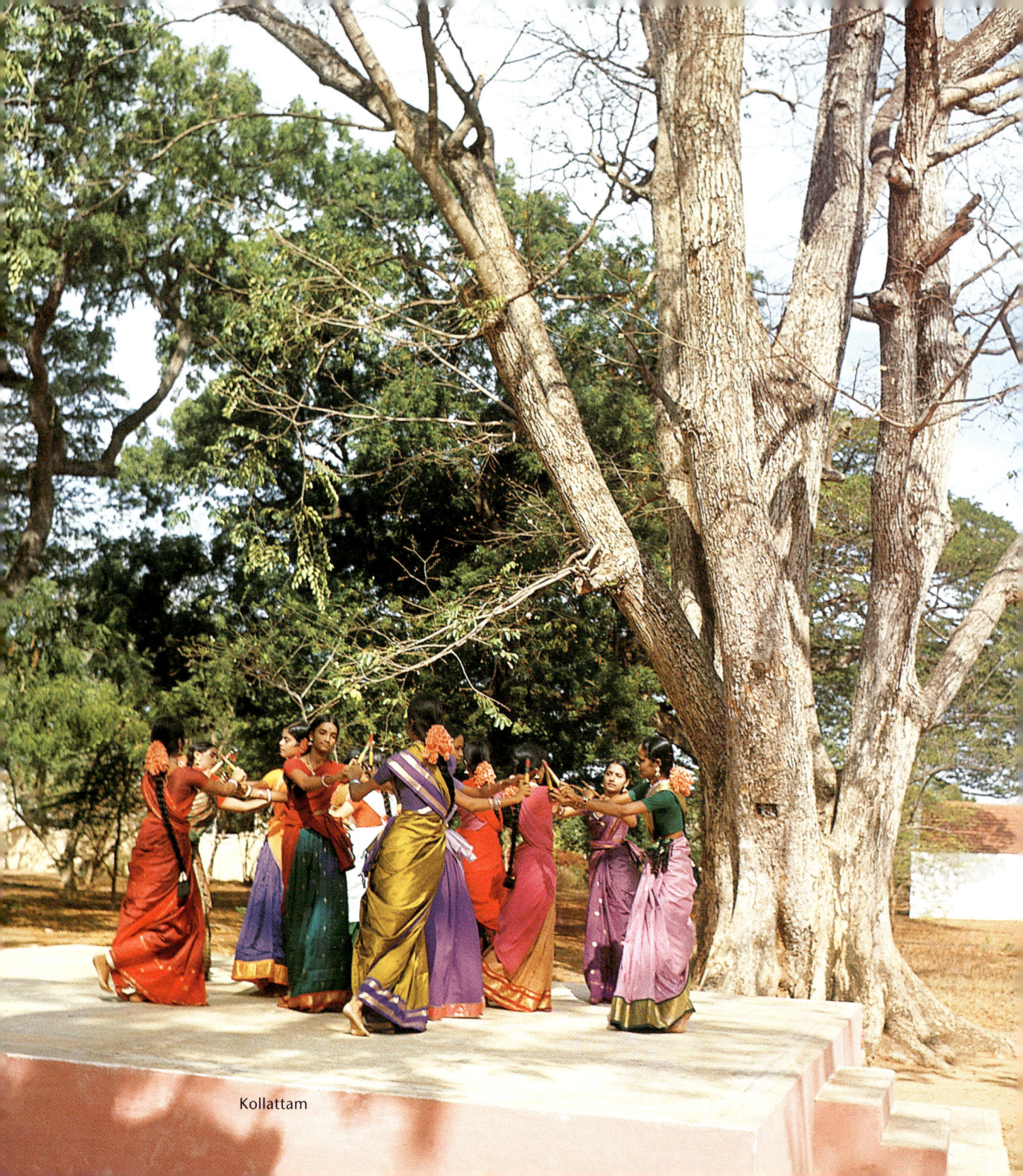

Kollattam

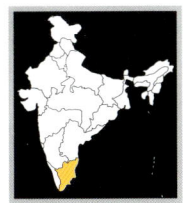

t w e l v e

TAMIL NADU

The land of classical music (Carnatic) and dance (Bharatanatyam) also boasts of a plethora of folk dance forms. Located strategically facing the Bay of Bengal, this state on the southeastern coast of India is steeped in tradition and rich in culture.

Kavadi is the most famous folk dance style of Tamil Nadu. Funnily enough, in addition to the rustic people whose show this is, a part of the police force is specially selected and trained to showcase the dance! Kavadi is dedicated to God Murugan, son of Shiva. The dancers balance upon their heads elaborate bamboo contraptions stuck with peacock feathers and flowers. Such is their skill and focus that they dance without holding or even touching their loads. Not only that, the dancers build up a tempo and often end up in a frenzy of movement (without disturbing the bamboo structures) to give a suitably difficult and impressive display to please and propitiate Murugan.

Karagam is akin to Kavadi but in place of bamboo structures, the dancers use metal pots or *karagams*. The dance is dedicated to Goddess Mariamman, who wards off calamities.

Moharram

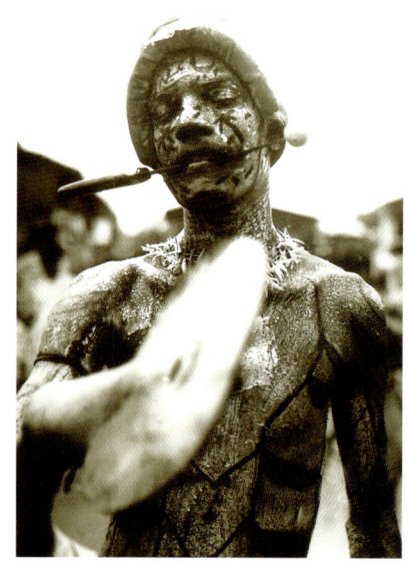

Moharram is an important event for Shia Muslims, who observe this ten-day ritual period to commemorate the martyrdom of Hassan and Hussain, grandsons of Prophet Mohammad. The participants pierce their bodies — sometimes their tongues as well — with small arrows and publicly undergo other forms of self-flagellation while dancing in a spiritual frenzy.

Oyil Attam hails from the Madurai-Trichy-Coimbatore region. The costume looks alien to the region — shiny pants teamed with decorative vests and a much-flourished handkerchief — but the dancing is very much of this place, with plenty of energetic movement and revelry. The dummy-horse version is called **Puravi Attam**.

Bhootam presents to folk gatherings at fairs or *melas* a look at popular characters like the village money-lender and snake charmers through dummy shells which the dancers, all young boys, sport on the upper half of their bodies. The dummies, made of cardboard and coloured paper, give the dancers added height.

Kai Silambu is performed by male dancers on festive occasions. A hollow metal ring is used to keep the rhythm. This dance is often staged in temples, too.

Kollattam is a dance for all seasons and events and is performed by women. It has three versions. In the eponymous form, the dancers hold small wooden rods. In the **Kummi** style, the women clap their hands while dancing in a circle. In the **Pinnal,** rods are fastened to ribbons or ropes suspended from a tall central pole or a higher point and the dancers weave patterns as they move. Obviously, it requires some expertise as one false move

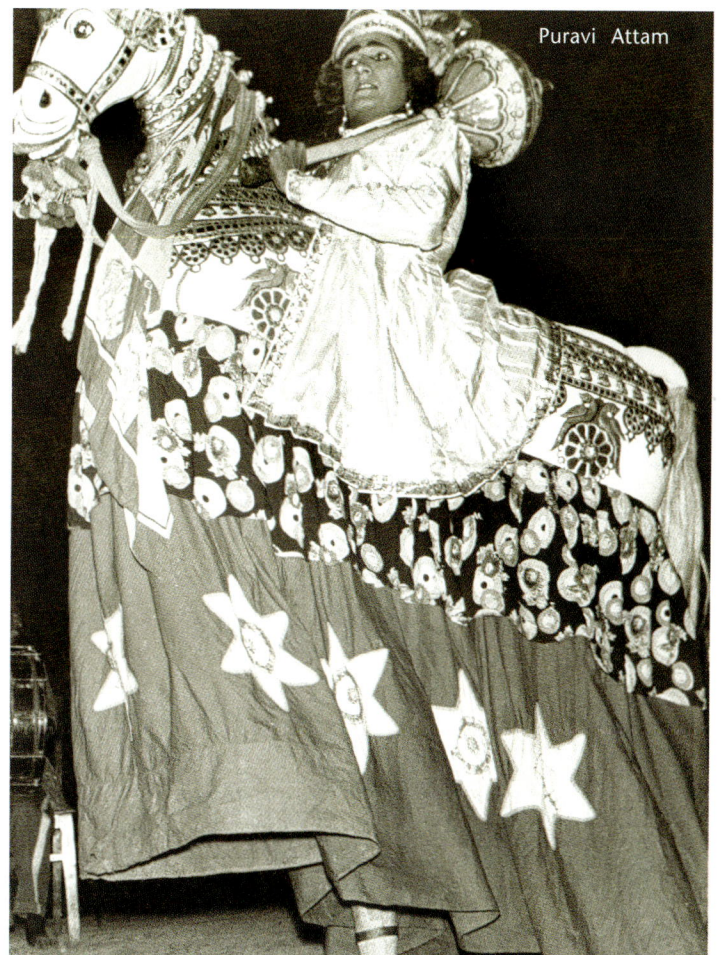

Puravi Attam

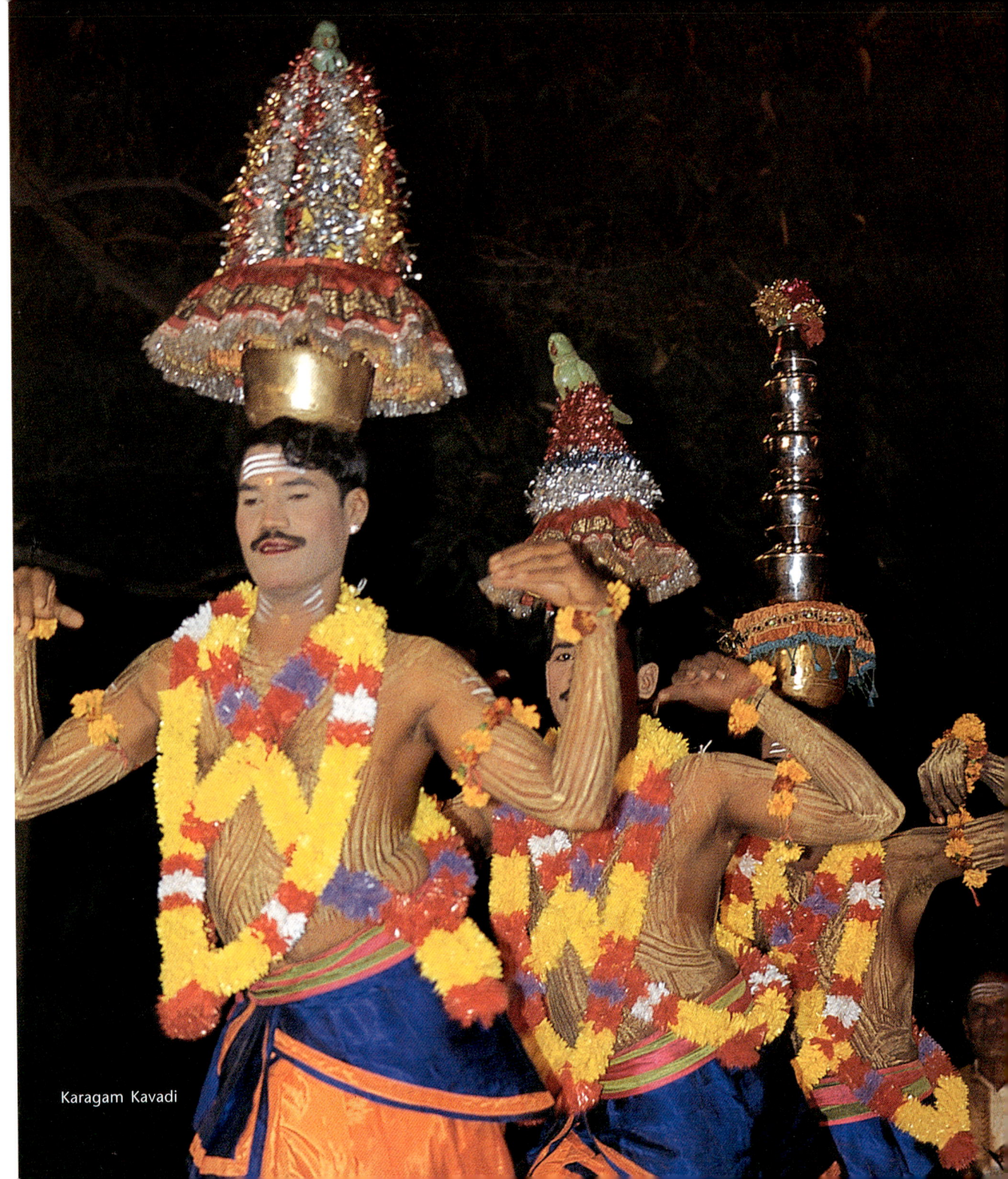

Karagam Kavadi

or one wrong tug could upset the whole delicate edifice. The gaily-dyed ribbons look pretty as they are braided and unbraided as the women dance in unison, taking measured steps.

Theru Koothu, meaning street play, is the well-loved folk theatre of Tamil Nadu. It begins with an invocation to Lord Ganesha, the god who removes all obstacles from one's path, to ensure that the performance takes place smoothly and successfully. Often, it is the famous episode from the *Mahabharata* that tells of the disrobing of Draupadi by Duryodhana, which is enacted in a very stylised manner. Mostly, trained men play all the roles.

Kurathis are the gypsy dancers often associated with fortune-telling and hold an important place in traditional lore (Kuravanjis) of Tamil Nadu.

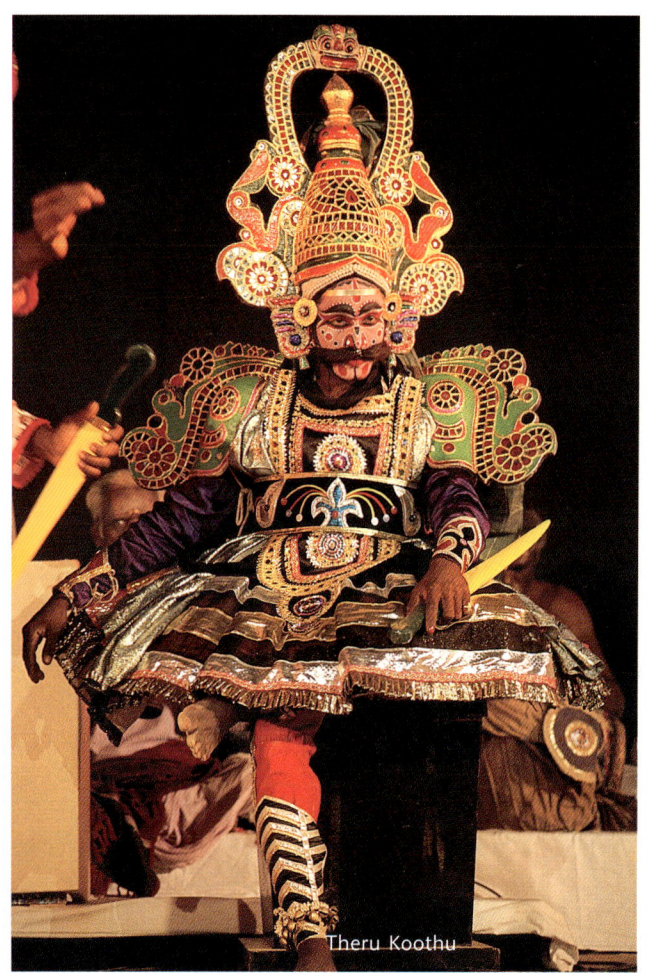

Theru Koothu

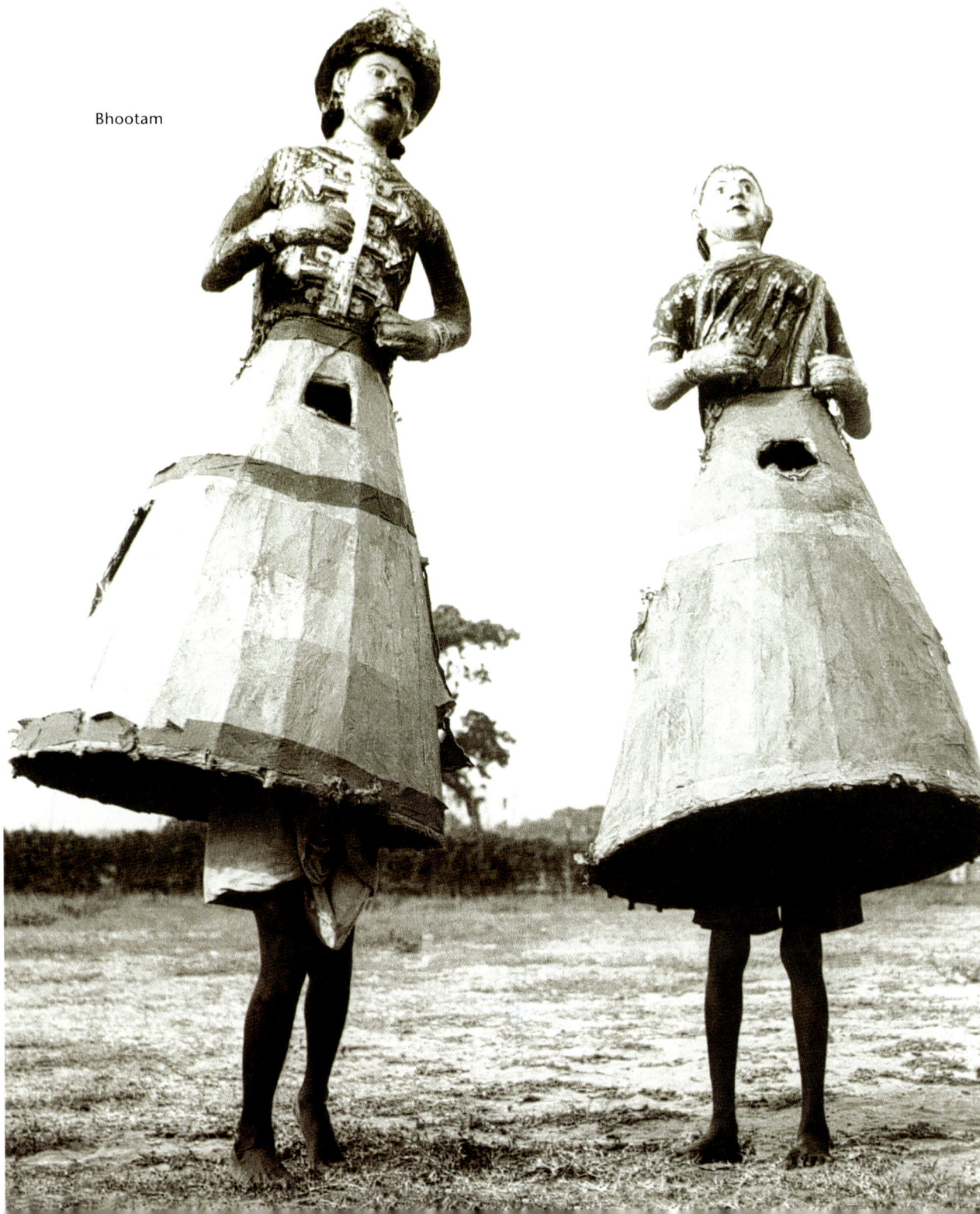

Bhootam

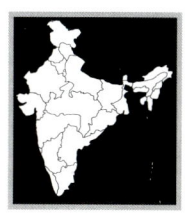

t h i r t e e n

PONDICHERRY

ondicherry, formerly a French colony, has several indigenous dances performed by men. Of these, the **Podikazhi Attam**, which is performed by a group of stick-wielding fishermen, is the most well known one. Lusty singing and a lot of merrymaking and clapping are in order. The simple and spontaneous fishermen need hardly any excuse to dance, and certainly not when the day's catch has been plentiful.

Bhootam is the dummy-dancers who take to the streets in a jovial procession to mark festivities and weddings. The idea of such a disguise is to ward off evil spirits.

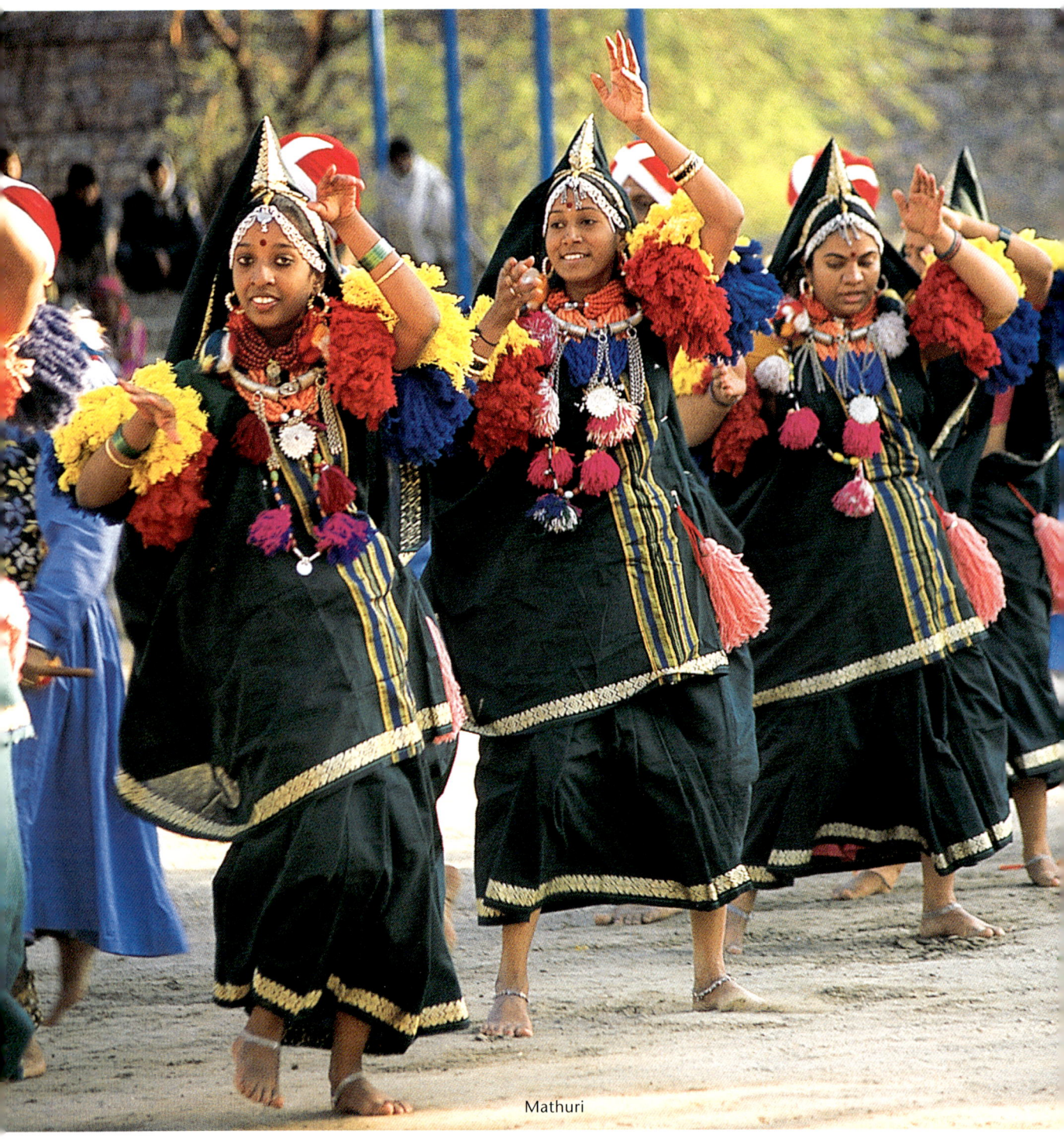

Mathuri

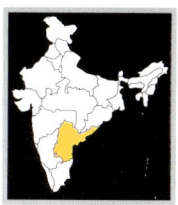

f o u r t e e n

ANDHRA PRADESH

Andhra Pradesh is the meeting point of the cultures of North and South India. Its people are passionate about their land and its customs. They are open-spirited and share their wealth of culture generously. Many of the classical traditions here (for example, *Yakshagana Kuchipudi*) originated from folk culture. The folk forms, including the dances, manifest a mellow richness of style and substance, the result of a symbiotic co-existence of the gypsies and the gentry.

The **Lambadi** dance of the gypsies of Andhra is common in the Telengana region. It is the most important folk dance of the state and is performed by women alone. Gypsy women wearing their distinctive chunky silver jewellery, dance the Lambadi with brass pots balanced on their heads.

Mathuri is danced by the eponymous tribe from Adilabad. Simple farm practices are woven into the structure of the dance. Men and women perform it separately. The purpose of the dance is to praise the tribal gods and war heroes.

Puli Vesham or Tiger Disguise is danced during Moharram by men wearing tiger costumes. The overall effect of the dance is electrifying, as there is a great deal of vibrancy, audacity, and invention in both the apparel and the group performance.

Poi Kal Kuthirai denotes a sham-legged horse, and this dance is a version of the horse-dummy dance of neighbouring Tamil Nadu. Dancers generally dance in pairs, one man and one woman, and regale the audience at weddings and festivals.

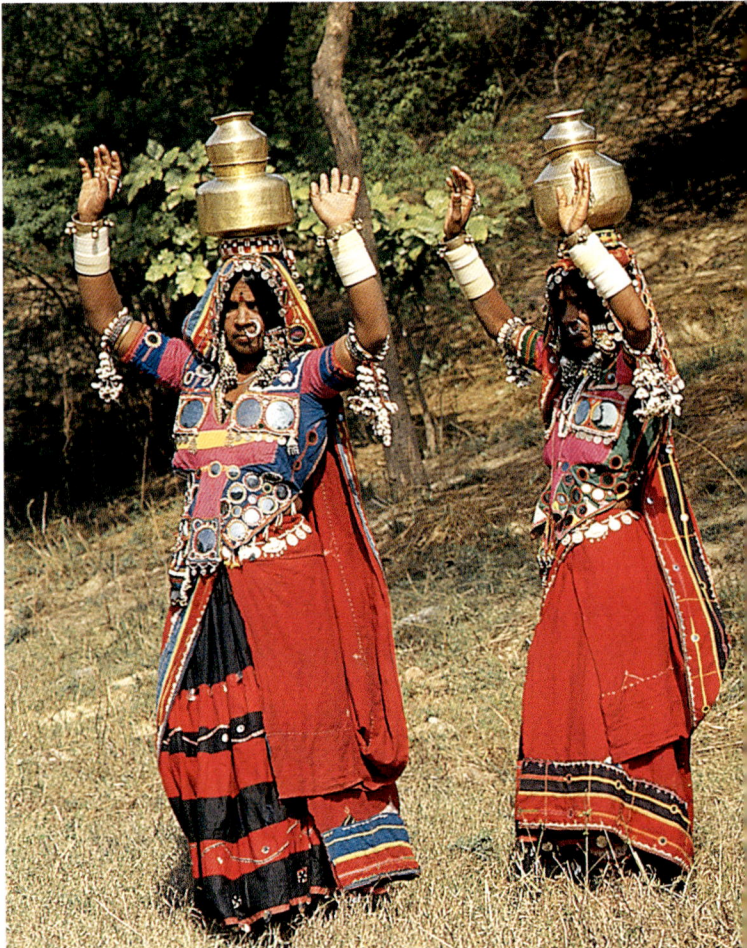

Lambadi

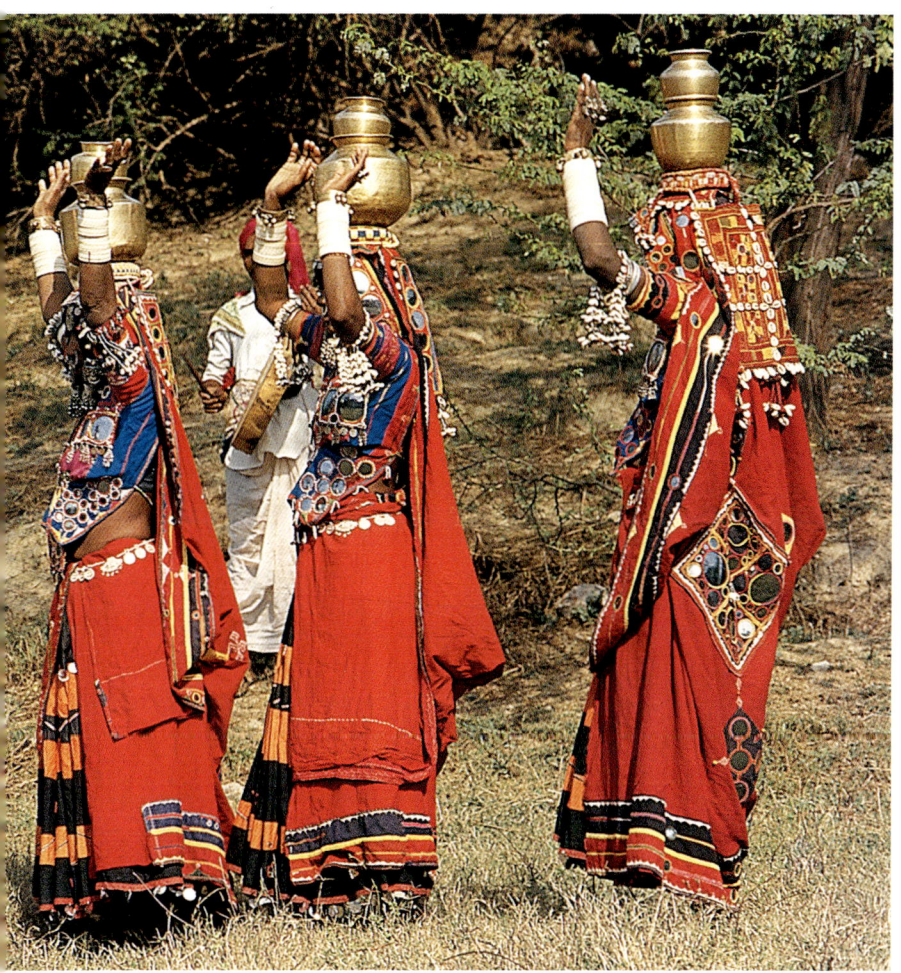

Gosadi is the principal dance form of the Gond tribe of Andhra Pradesh, performed as a votive offering. The dancers, mostly men, adorn themselves with forest products, like nuts and berries, and wear headgear bright with peacock plumes.

Toorpu Bhagvatam is one of the folk-drama styles of Andhra. The ever-popular tale of Krishna and Satyabhama is the mainstay of this act. Unfortunately, this is a fast vanishing style, as very few perform it today.

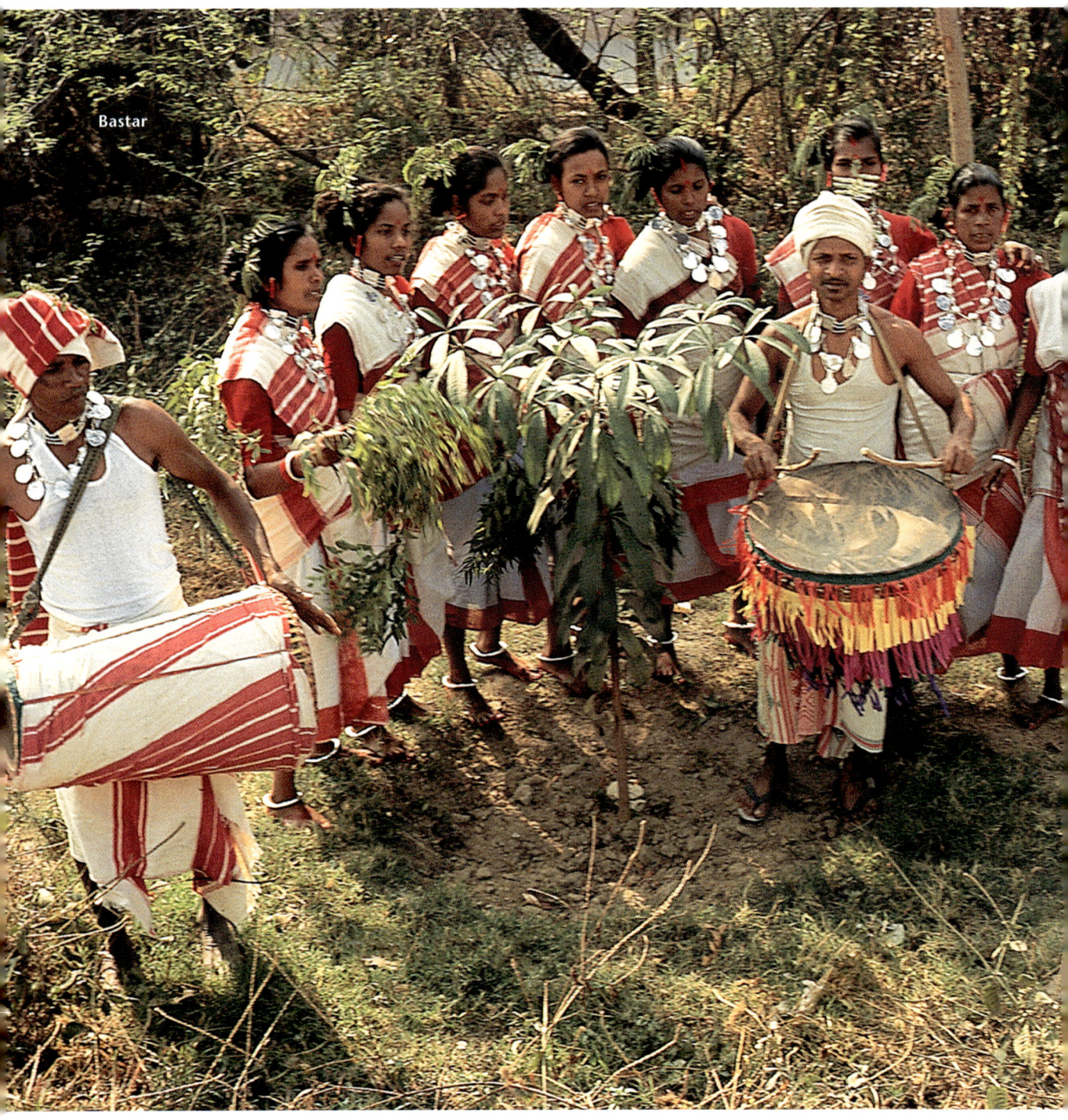

Bastar

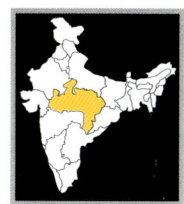

f i f t e e n

MADHYA PRADESH

Ravines and dacoits, dungeons and devils abound in such is the stuff of the popular folklore surrounding Madhya Pradesh, situated on the central plateau of India. It is the largest state in terms of landmass and some of the best known tribal cultures (like Bastar) of the country are found here. The Madhya Pradeshis are unassertive, talented, and cultured and they dance on practically every occasion of life! The individuality of the many tribes living here reveals the cultural variety that exists in the state.

The **Gaur** dance is based on bison hunt. The Maria Gonds of Bastar adorn their heads with bison horns while performing this dance. The Bastar region is central to the cultural entity of Madhya Pradesh in every sense of the word, and the Maria Gonds are born dancers.

Mandri is danced by boys belonging to the Muria tribe of Bastar. They dance while playing the drum. The steps are complicated as the boys kneel, jump, gyrate, and do everything their nimble bodies allow them to do while dancing.

Jawara is the harvest dance of women of the Bundelkhand region. They bear on their heads baskets containing the jawar crop. The dancers are gaily attired and wear heavy silver jewellery.

Morni, celebrates the advent of the seasons, especially rain and spring.

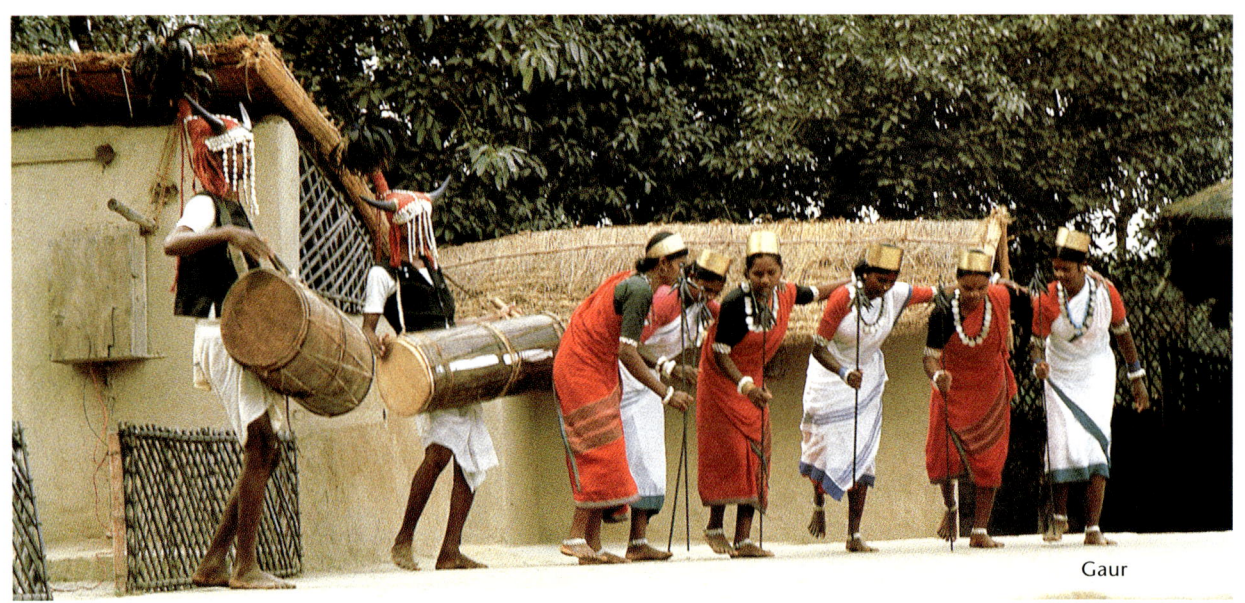

Gaur

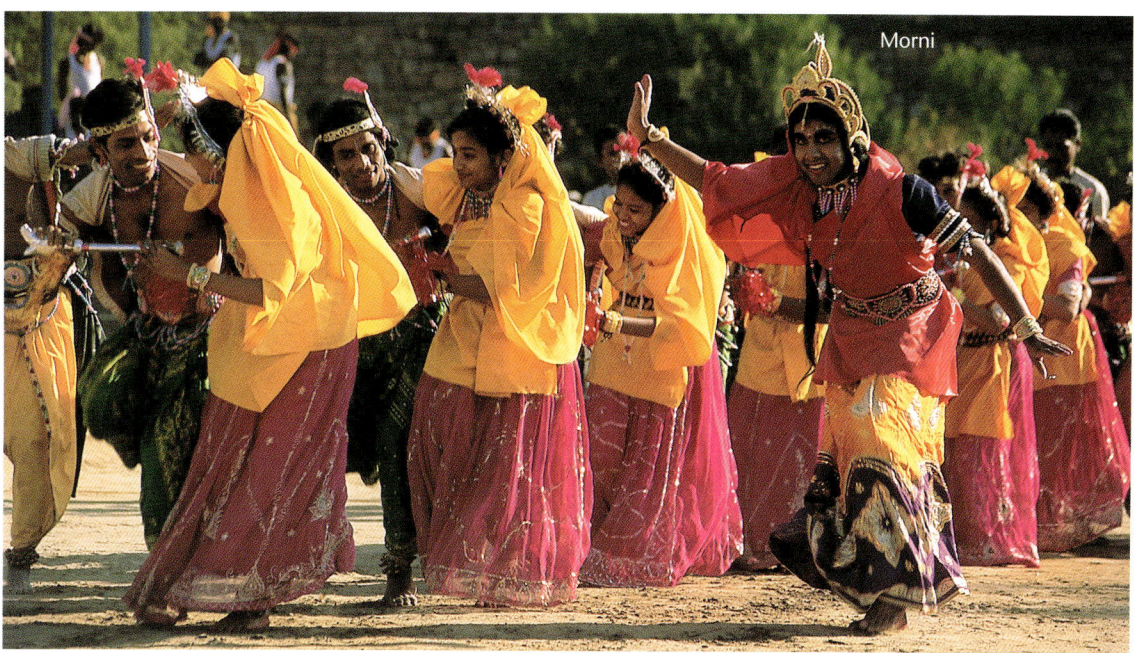

Morni

Maach is a type of folk drama having a heavy dance component. It is performed by men, who essay the female roles too. The proceedings have an unmistakable flavour of Rajasthani culture. Sword-wielding macho men narrate tales of warriors and kings while demure women (who are actually men) add allure and glamour with their dainty ways and attractive costumes. *Maach* follows rather strict stage ethics, with each character performing an invocatory item and then ritualistically cleaning the stage before the actual performance begins.

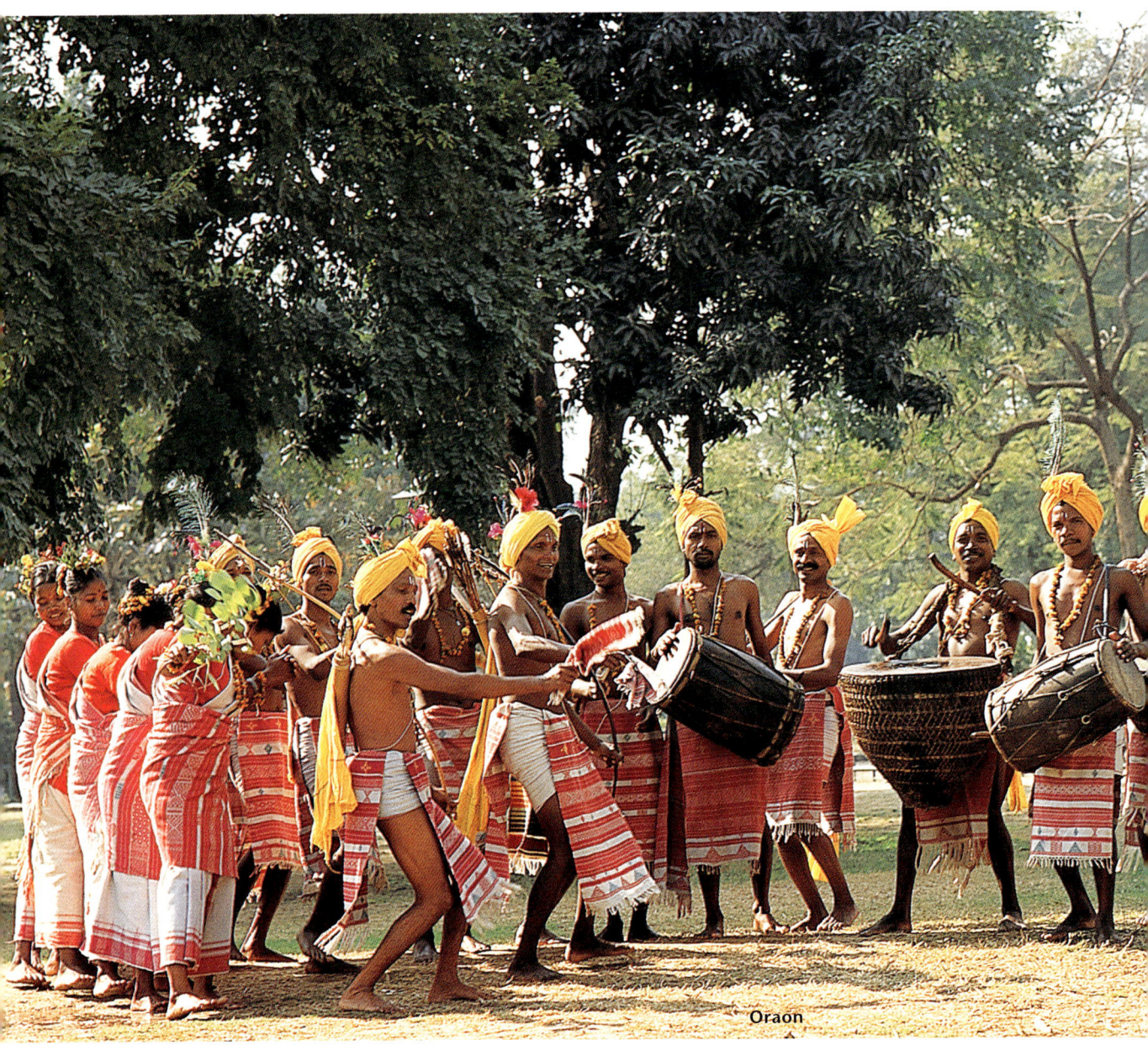

Oraon

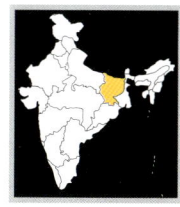

BIHAR

The land of the Buddha is also known for its mélange of folk cultures. All of them celebrate the changing cycle of seasons and nature. Dances linked to harvesting and sowing form an integral part of the folk tradition of the state that is rich in minerals and boasts of enormous natural wealth. The people of Bihar are a spirited lot. They uphold their own exuberance and zest for living, and their character and attitude find a focused manifestation in their folk dance forms.

The **Brindabani** is performed during Chaitra Parva, the week-long festival marking the onset of spring. It has a religious overtone. The performer is a worshipper who dresses up in an outfit fashioned out of twigs and leaves to represent the monkey-god Hanuman, around whom the dance revolves.

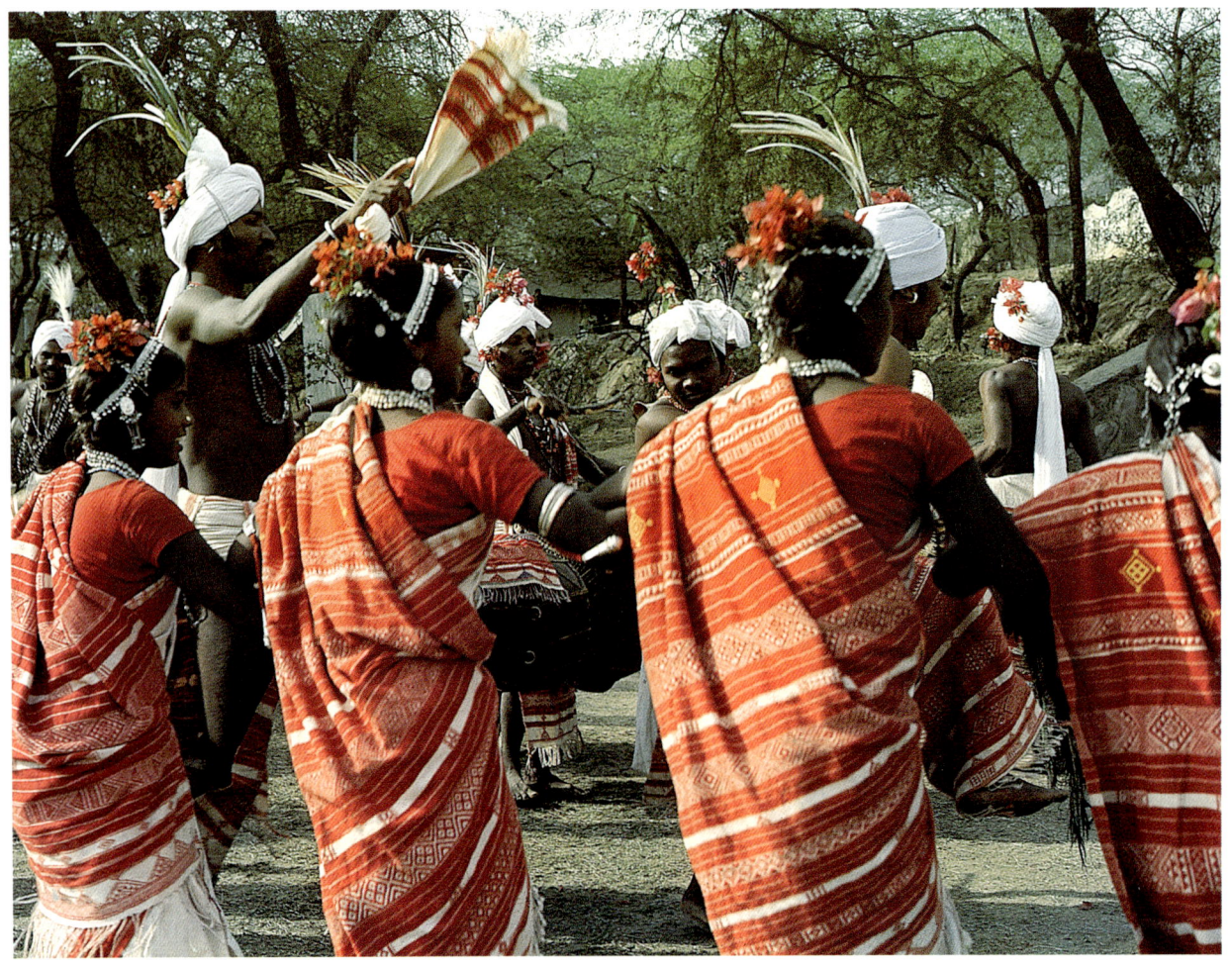

opp. Santhals

The **Oraon** is the dance of the Oraon tribals, who form an important design in the mosaic of Bihar's indigenous cultures. In this lively and closely coordinated dance, which allows subtle changes within a given pattern, the women perform while the men play the drum.

The **Santhals** are another important tribal group of Bihar, and their dance, to the accompaniment of hypnotic drumbeats, is for many Indians the archetypal tribal dance. The backbreaking grind of their daily lives gives them toned, sculpted figures. They wear simple costumes with style and adorn their hair with headdresses or simply a bunch of bright flowers. Their delivery is extremely polished; every dancer in the group maintains a perfect sync with everyone else.

Mangala Ghat is performed by the Ho tribe of the Singhbhum region. Women carry pots on their heads and dance to the beats of a huge drum. The performers fall into a trance when the dancing reaches its peak tempo.

Jatra Ghat, **Kalika Ghat,** and **Garia Ghat** are all forms of folk dance associated with the Chaitra Parva or the spring festivities. While in the Jatra Ghat the dancers wear red, in the Kalika style, they wear black and carry pots on their heads. In the Garia variation, the pots are suspended from the dancers' shoulders.

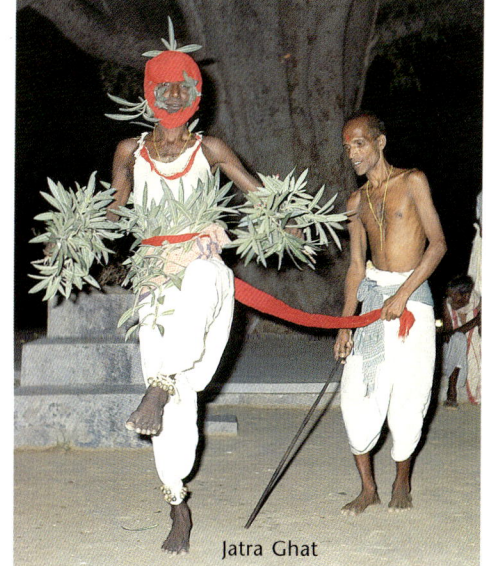

Jatra Ghat

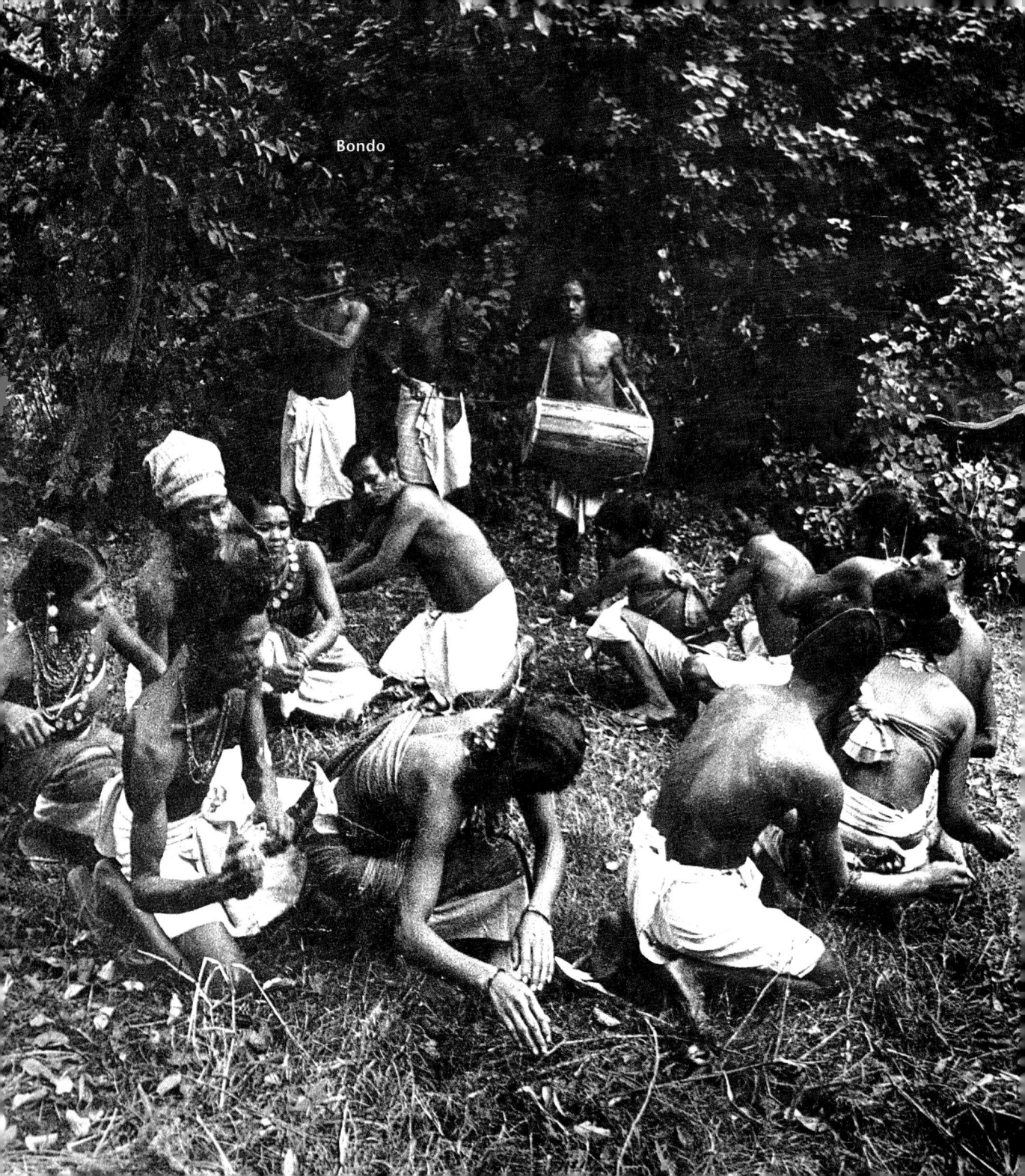

Bondo

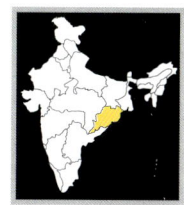

s e v e n t e e n

ORISSA

Our journey now brings us to the land of poets and *patachitra* paintings, temples and talismans, Kalinga and culture. Orissa is full of monuments, magic, and mysticism. Several centuries of layered history have vested it with a kaleidoscope of folk forms. The Oriyas have a close link with Mother Earth and her various manifestations. Orissa boasts of both an active classical and a glorious folk tradition.

The **Dalkhai** dance of the Sambalpur region is performed by women at seasonal festivals. It is a feisty dance and the men join in by playing on the drums and other assorted instruments.

Karma is another popular dance form of Orissa that is performed in honour of Karamsani, the deity believed to control fate. The style is often also associated with the worship of new plants or saplings to ensure a good crop.

Bondo is bonding with a difference! Eligible girls and boys belonging to the Bondo tribe of Koraput marry only after spending a ritual night together to find out whether they are compatible. The Bondos dance after the village elders solemnise this ceremony. It is the women who dance while the men play the drums – or second fiddle!

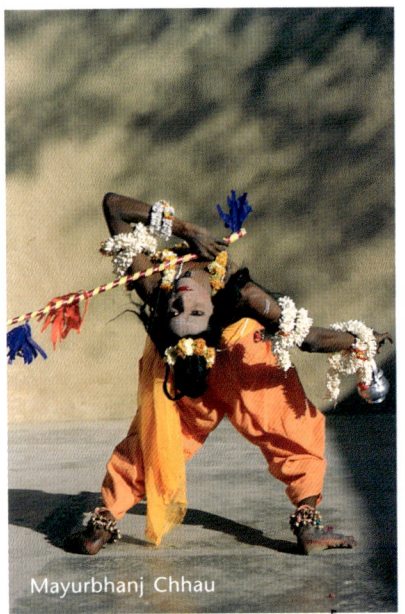

Mayurbhanj Chhau

Keertan is a song and dance routine of the Vaishnav cult. The Vaishnavs have been a part of Oriya culture since the tenth century. Cymbals, drums, and vocals accompany much dancing as deities are taken out on a ceremonial procession.

Chaiti Ghori is a version of the dummy-horse dance but in Orissa it is danced by the fisher-folk. Only men undertake the dance and sing songs that are full of mirth and merrymaking, with an element of humour.

Mayurbhanj Chhau uses mythology to depict legend and lores of the region. This is the only form of Chhau which does not use mask.

Paik was originally a dance performed by the militia (*paik*) of native rulers. It was conceived to show off the militia's preparedness for defence as well as offence and no doubt it gave great joy to the kings for whom it used to be staged. In its present-day manifestation, this dance relieves the stress (and boredom) of policing and army duties as well as ordinary lives.

Ghoomra derives its form and meaning from the drum bearing the same name. Men and boys essay this form during festive events. It calls for a lot of stamina and skill to dance and play the drum at the same time.

Ranappa literally means stilts, and this style is actually performed on stilts. It is danced by young boys who are expert enough to perform dance steps while keeping their precarious balance on their stilts.

Nian Pata, **Kanta Pata,** and **Jhula Pata** are versions of the same rituals performed during Chaitra Parva in neighbouring Bihar. *The Nian Pata* is danced on embers and the *Kanta Pata* on a bed of thorns. In the Jhula Pata style, the performer's feet are tied to a horizontal beam or log and he hangs upside-down over a fire. The last form, obviously, is more of an endurance test than a dance!

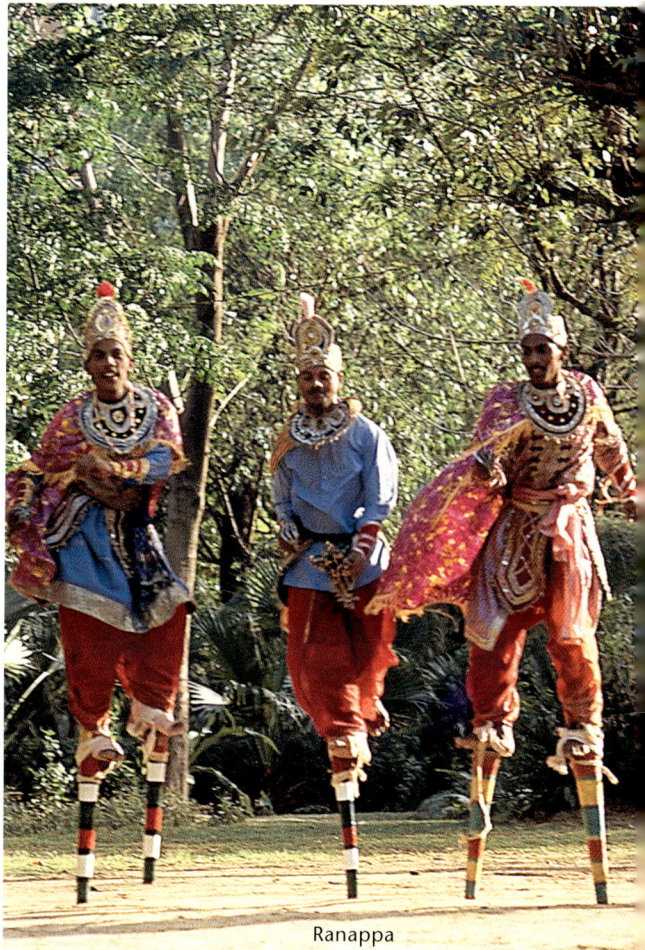
Ranappa

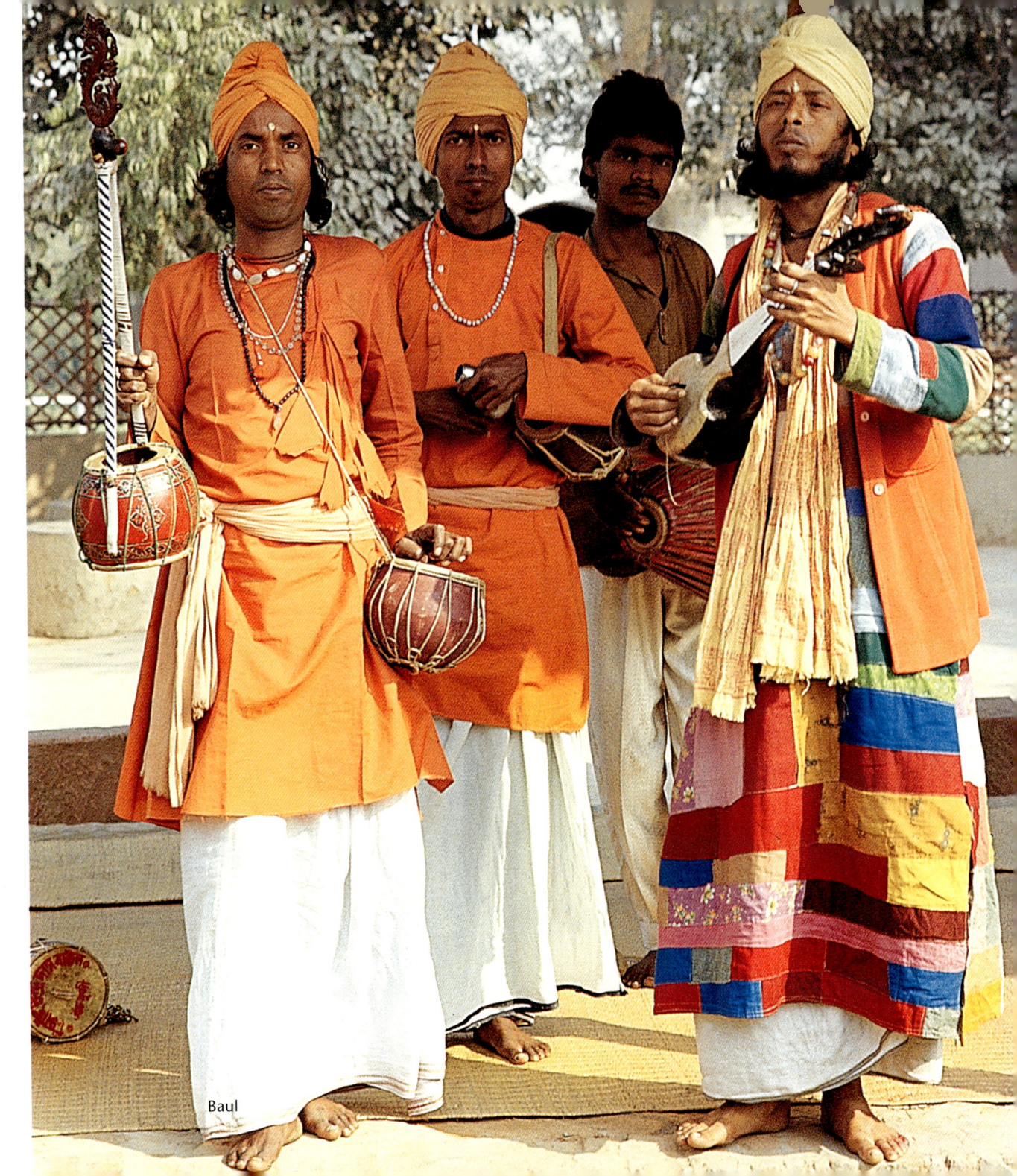

Baul

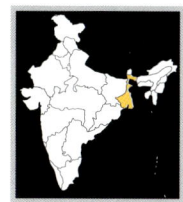

e i g h t e e n

WEST BENGAL

*H*ere the land meets the eternal sea, the Bay of Bengal. Slow rivers widen into deltas and estuaries. There are forests and mangroves, and resplendent lush green low-lying fields. Mother Nature in all her glory and fury hugs this land of poets and patriots, singers and scientists, educationists and economists. This is the land of literary greats and cinematic giants and a people proud of their history and heritage.

Bolan is performed at Gajan, a festival observed in spring to worship and honour Shiva. Men wear garish attires and masquerade as women, dancing and singing the *Bolan*.

Kali Nach is also performed at the Gajan festival but it honours not Shiva but Kali, the great female energy that destroys evil. She is

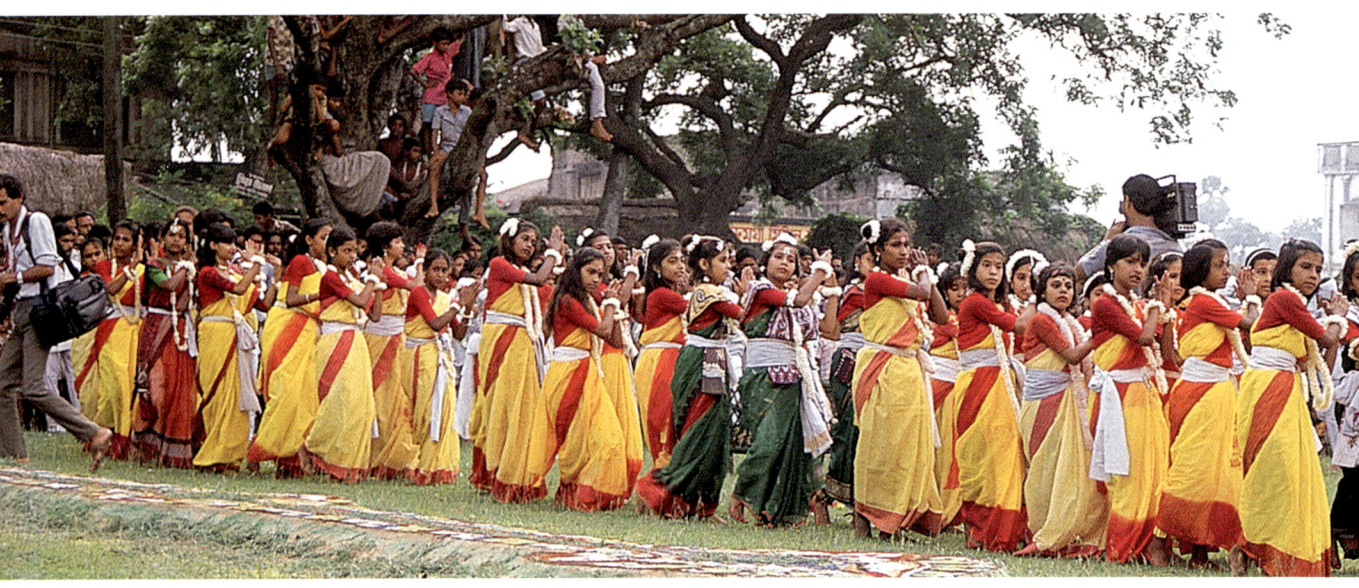

Santiniketan's Basanta

represented in idols as a dark or black complexioned goddess, with long untied coal-black tresses covering her unclad body, and wearing a garland of skulls. Hindu mythology says that the predominance of evil in the world made Kali go on a rampage. It was Shiva, her consort, who finally calmed her by lying down in her way. She stepped on him and stuck out her tongue in shame. Kali is greatly worshipped in Bengal. In the *Kali Nach*, the performer wears a black mask signifying the goddess and purifies the stage before starting the show. The ritualistic dance mimes the great fury of Kali.

Basanta is performed at Santiniketan on the occasion of Basant Panchami (advent of spring).

Baul is the dance of the wandering minstrels of rural Bengal. These minstrels, their songs and their dance, are all called Baul. They play the *ektara*, a one-stringed drone instrument, and dance ecstatically in praise of Nature and its Keeper.

Raibenshe was originally danced with spears, not surprising, as the performers (like the Paiks in Orissa) were soldiers retained by the zamindars of Bengal. The soldiers themselves developed this dance form. Obviously, it is performed now more as an entertainment than for any other purpose.

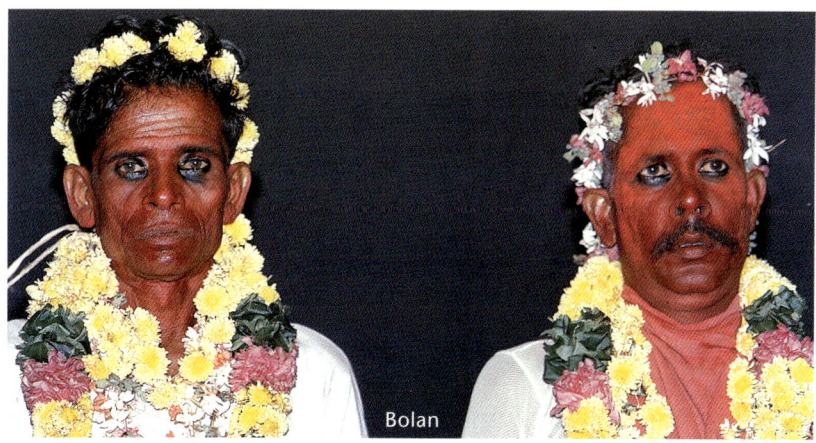

Bolan

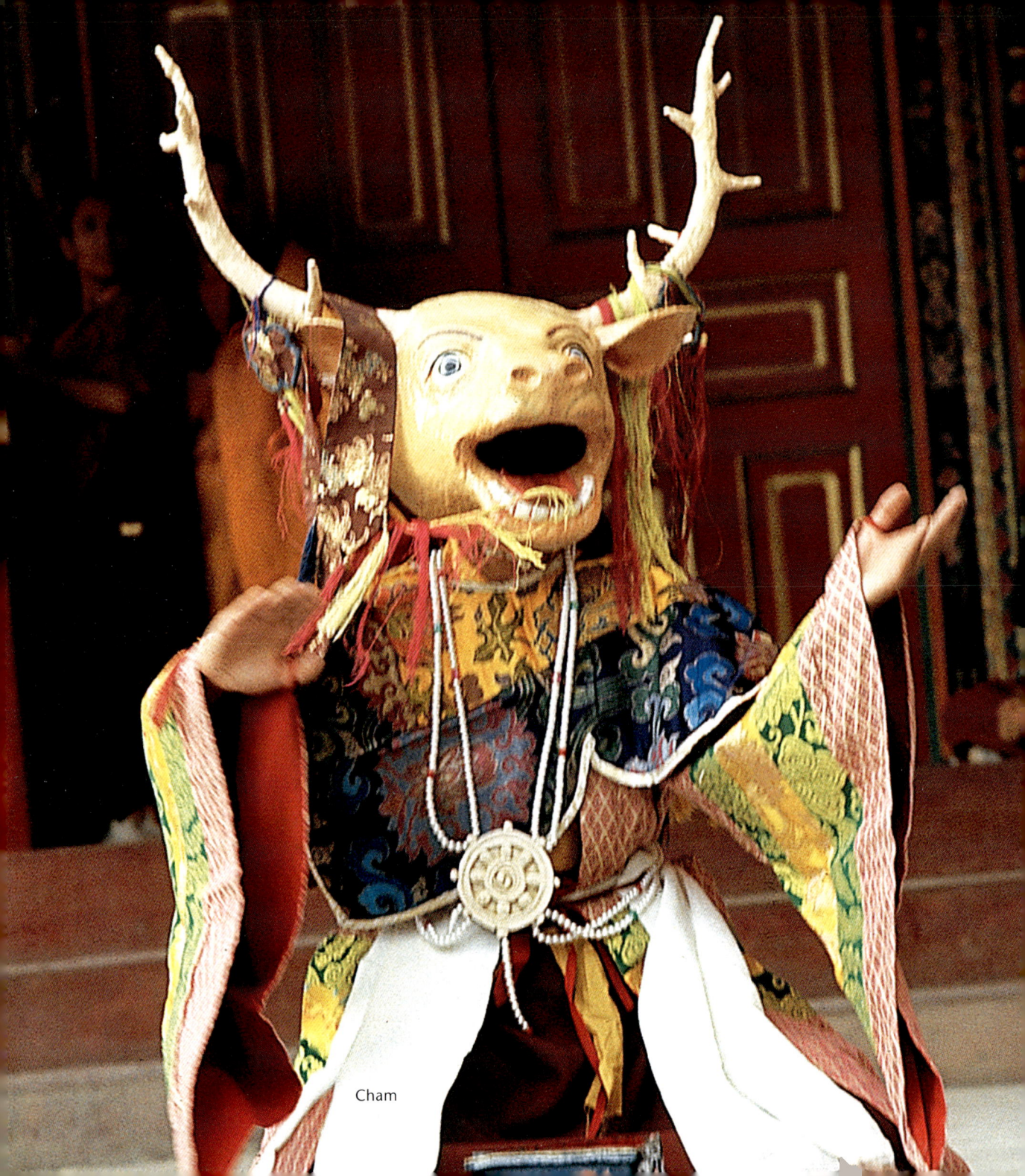

Cham

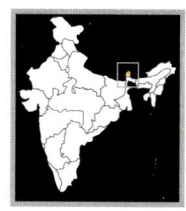

n i n e t e e n

SIKKIM

Sikkim is one of the "seven sisters" of the north-east that joined the Indian Union. This erstwhile Himalayan kingdom has a unique culture and many cults derived from Buddhist traditions. The sturdy and silent men, strong but sweet women, and wide-eyed, innocent youngsters of Sikkim reflect a serenity that can only mean peace within – in the heart – as well as peace outside.

Cham is the most popular of Sikkimese folk dance forms and involves the wearing of huge masks and dancing to ward off evil spirits on the occasion of the Tibetan New Year, the Sikkimese New Year, and other festivals.

The **Shanag** or Black Hat Dance is a slow and languorous dance style performed by monastic men. The accompanying song recounts tales of mysticism in a language that only the initiated can understand. The dance has a great deal of variation in mood and is awe-inspiring and at the same time, engaging.

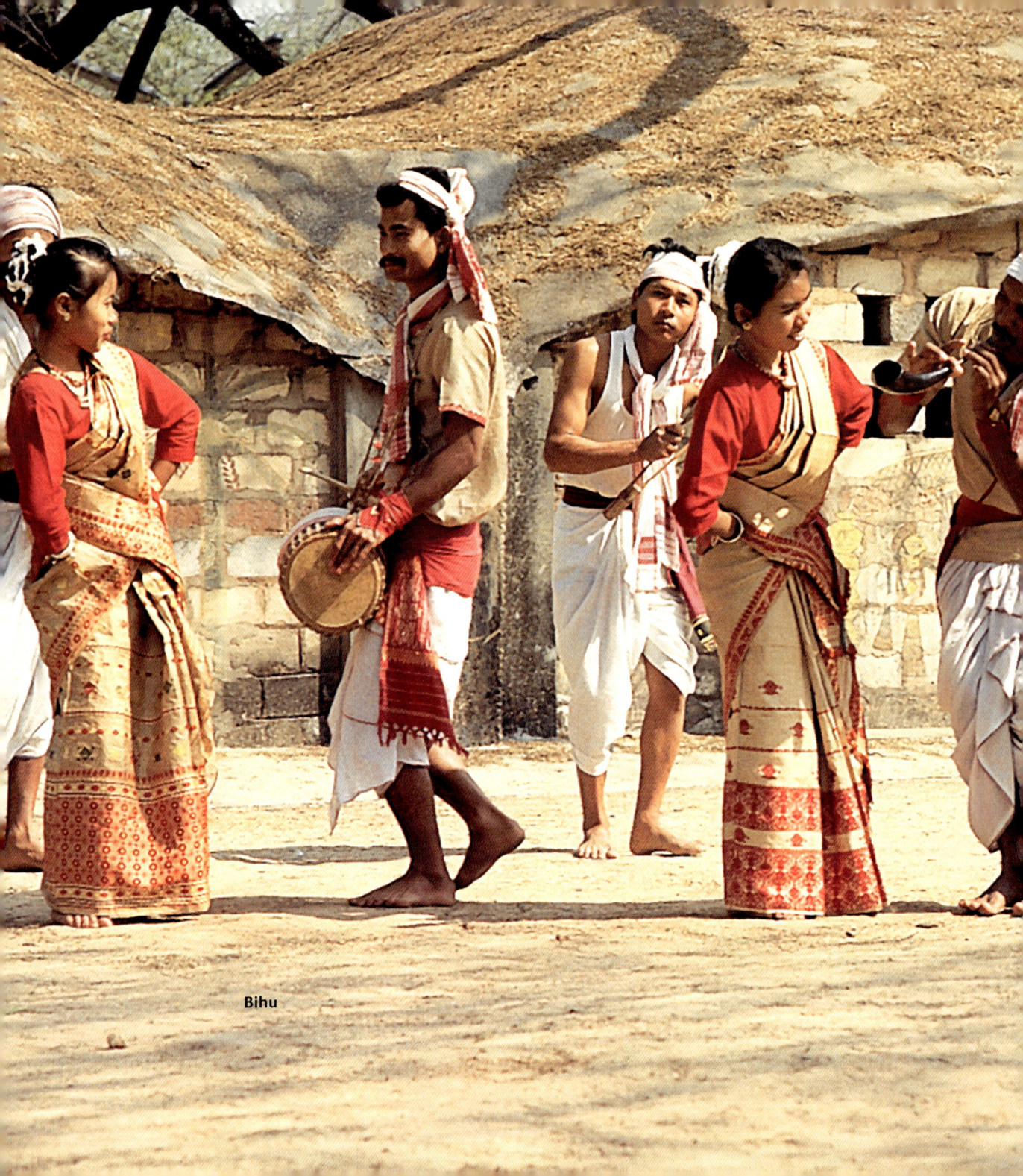

Bihu

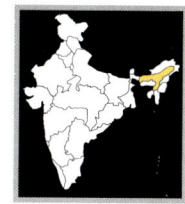

t w e n t y

Assam

The green of tea estates, the azure of clear skies – these two colours well represent a people who believe their origin is closely linked to Mother Nature and celebrate every generous gift given by her. The people of Assam, gentle and cultured, are unique in that they seem to live only to dance.

Bihu represents the unbridled spirit of the Assamese people. The dance is a part of the Bohag Bihu festival that is observed in mid-April, when harvesting is under way. Both men and women take part in it. Bihu is as much a grand social occasion as it is a celebratory rite, and the Bihu dance, especially the one performed by splendidly groomed women, has a lively element of flirtation and raillery.

Bou Nach was a customary dance by a young bride. She had to perform in front of her new family to show her skills and be judged and evaluated. This custom has slowly faded out, and not surprisingly so.

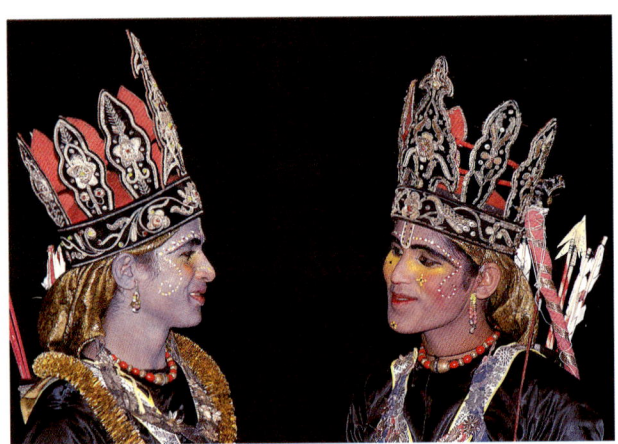

Ankia Nat

Deodhani is a ritual dance in honour of the serpent-goddess Manasa. The dancer, by tradition, remains unmarried and celibate. Men play cymbals, gradually increasing the tempo, and the performer is expected to dance into a frenzy.

Behula enacts the popular legend of Behula, a woman who opposed and fought Goddess Manasa to bring her husband Lakhindar back from the dead. The performer is a man dressed as a woman and he plays both Behula and Manasa. While depicting Manasa, he gyrates and twists his body like a snake, a feat that never fails to impress his audience. A band of drummers makes the music.

Ankia Nat is a ritual dance drama performed only by celibate monks who live in *satras* or monasteries. The monks sing and dance in praise of Lord Krishna or enact themes from the *Ramayana*. The leader (*sutradhar*) also dances while conducting the ritual.

Ojapali is yet another ritual tradition of Assam. It presents tales from mythology through song and a minimalist dance, having simple gestures and mime. Generally, the performers are in a team of six or more.

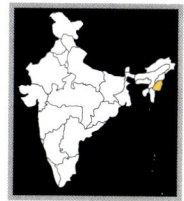

t w e n t y o n e

MANIPUR

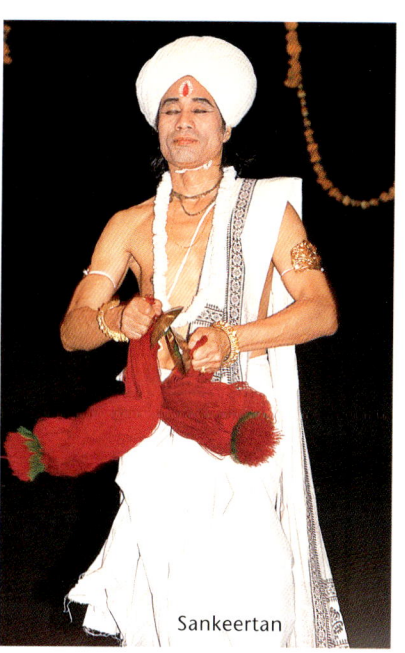

Sankeertan

The legend that surrounds Manipur's name is as sparkling as the name itself, one of those droll vignettes that humanise the immortals and endear them to ordinary people. Parvati was entranced when she saw Krishna disporting with the *gopis* in the pastoral paradise of Vraj. So she importuned her own lord, Shiva, to create a gem of a country for their own pleasure and sport. Shiva deputed his serpent-king to locate a suitable place. The reptile did find a lovely verdant valley, but it was dark and gloomy there. So the serpent-king hid a magnificent precious gem in its head that lit up the entire place while Shiva and Parvati danced. Hence the name Manipur or Gem Country. It is indeed a gem of a place where the people are extremely god-fearing and nature loving. The Manipuris

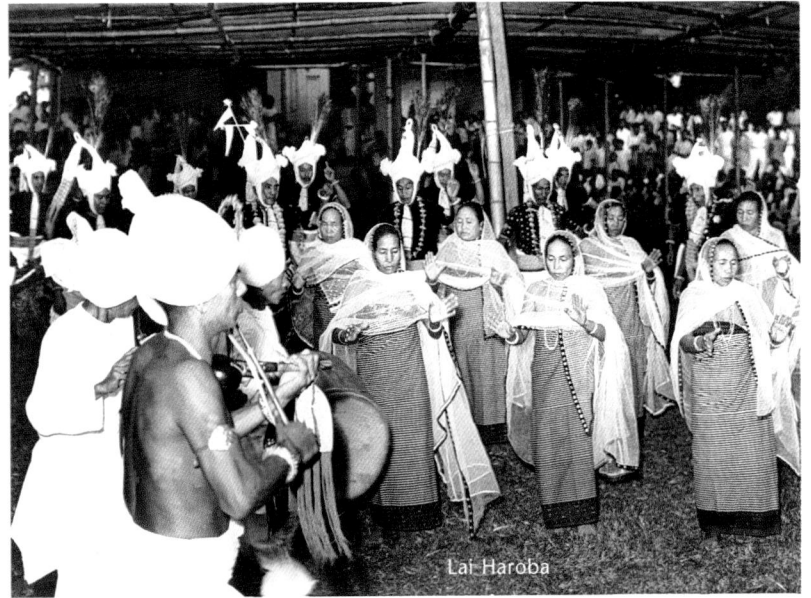

Lai Haroba

are also born dancers, with flexible bodies and a wonderful inherent understanding of grace and rhythm.

Thang-Ta, the martial dance of men brandishing swords and shields, is the most well-known dance form of Manipur. Men with agile, muscular bodies execute daring steps and swirl around, swords in hand. This is basically part of a combat regimen.

Dhol Cholom shows the centrality of drums (*dhol*) in Manipuri dance traditions. Different kinds of drums, ship-shaped and decorated for the special occasion, are pressed into service in this dance. Of course, the expert drummers also leap, dance, and display their superb athleticism while playing on their drums. Holi, the spring festival in which people smear each other with bright colours, is the time for the Dhol Cholom.

Thabal Chongi is a popular dance performed by both boys and girls. They join hands and sway gently and take infectious delight in this simple shared occasion.

The **Lai Haroba** presentation is both folk and classical in flavour. It is performed only at specific times and everyone, young and old alike, take part in the telling of the cherished folk tale of a princess and a soldier.

Sankeertan or congregational singing and dancing is typical of the Vaishnav cult. It is performed at births and weddings and also at the death of an elder. There are two styles of Sankeertan – Pung, which uses drums, and Kartal, where tasselled cymbals make their own distinctive clangour.

Holi, the festival of colours, is celebrated with much joy and impromptu dancing where no precise rules are followed. Men and women join in the merrymaking. At Imphal, the capital city, people converge at the temple of Govindji, which is the religious focal point.

Gop Raas or **Sanjeba** is a folk drama of Manipur. In this style, boys, all under ten years of age, perform and dance in praise of Krishna, the deity all Manipur worships. All the youthful dancers dress up like Krishna, wearing crowns adorned with peacock feathers, and carry flutes.

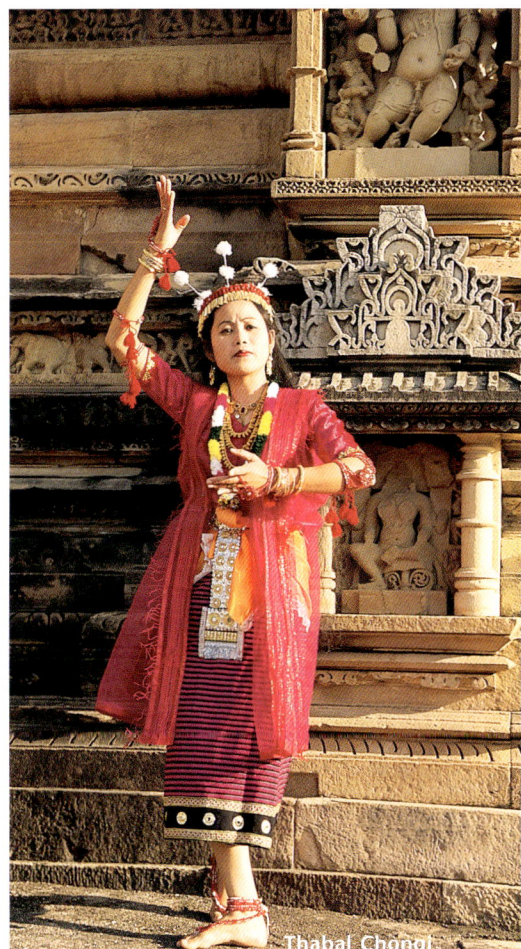

Thabal Chongi

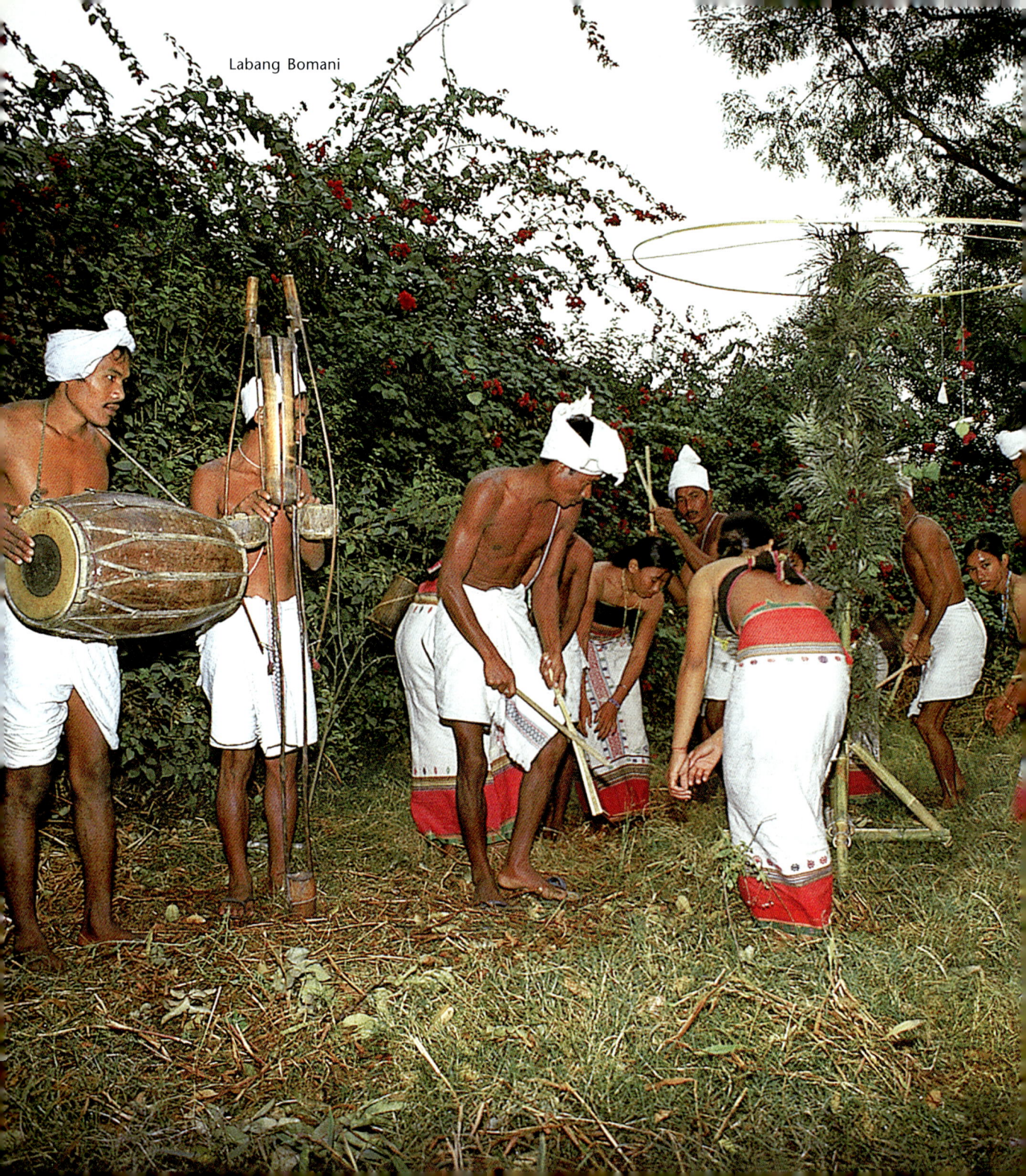

Labang Bomani

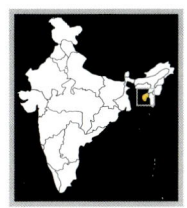

TRIPURA

*T*ripura is essentially a land of tribes. It is a serene and verdant paradise of sun-soaked valleys and rolling hills, forests, lakes, and waterfalls. The people of Tripura complete and complement this picture, as they are in total harmony with their setting.

Hajagiri is danced by young girls belonging to the Riang tribe. The Riangs worship both the tribal and the Hindu gods. The girls dance the *Hajagiri* to propitiate Goddess Lakshmi, who is believed to ensure prosperity.

Labang Bomani is perhaps the only dance in the world meant for insects! The dance is an ingenious homegrown mix of art and practical science. A particular insect species abounds at harvest time, and the Labang Bomani, though ostensibly a harvest dance, is actually geared towards catching these insects. Even the string instrument played during the dance makes a certain peculiar sound that attracts these insects!

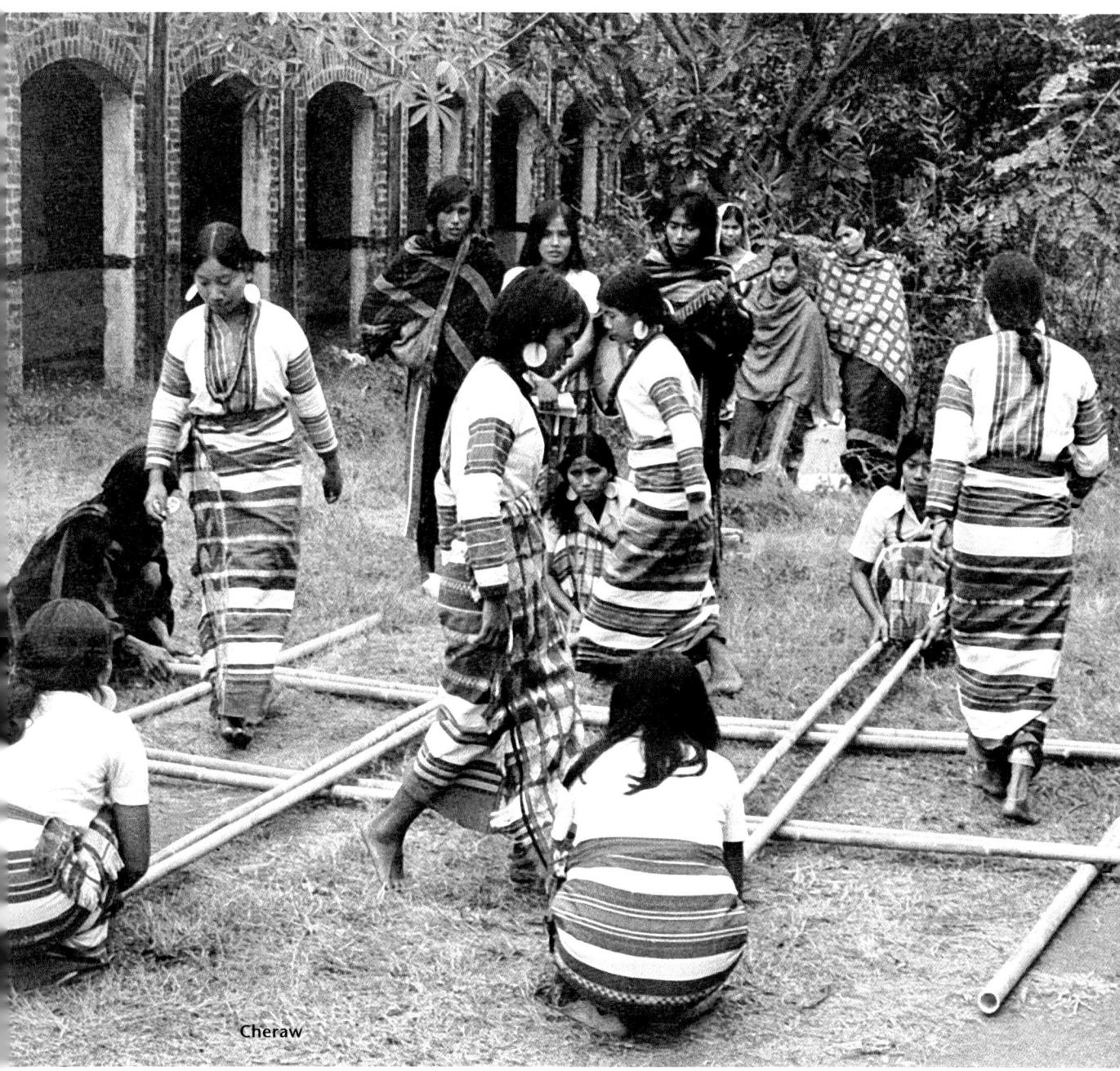

Cheraw

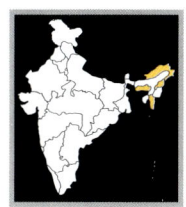

twenty three

OTHER NORTH-EASTERN STATES
(MIZORAM, MEGHALAYA, ARUNACHAL PRADESH & NAGALAND)

*B*ound by strong cultural links, the populace of each of these north-eastern states throbs with life and rhythm. Warriors by original vocation, several of the tribes living in the north-east use a wide variety of props while dancing, that bring to mind the essence of their heroic civilisation. The natural wealth of the region is only matched by the richness of their culture. The simple, honest, and brave hill people of the north-east are totally one with nature.

The **War Dances** performed by tribes like the Hill Miris, Tagnis, and Daflas of Arunachal Pradesh are an awesome sight. Wearing bulky headgears and elaborate costumes, the Daflas brandish swords and spears and present an electrifying demonstration of their skills. These dances enact various facets of combat.

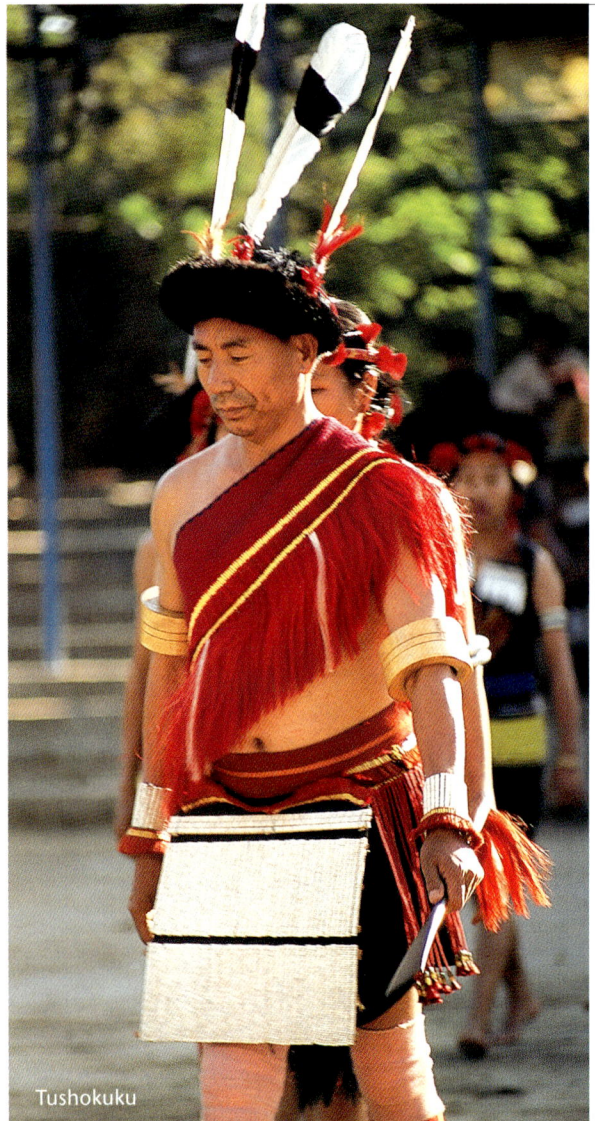
Tushokuku

The **Tushokuku** from Nagaland presents a mock combat. Most tribes in this state are known by the generic name Naga. Members of these tribes are born warriors. In this dance, precisely these instinctive combat skills are put on display. Interestingly, the dance may suddenly turn interactive so it calls for a high level of alertness from the spectators as well!

Cheraw or the Bamboo-Dance of Mizoram leaves a most lasting impression. Bamboo poles are arranged in a crisscross pattern on a large dance area. The performers, all girls, are divided into two groups. One group sits and claps the bamboo poles in a certain rhythm while the other group dances in steps to weave in and out of the space between the shifting bamboo poles.

Laho is a dance of the Jaintia Hills of Meghalaya. It was previously a ritual dance but is nowadays performed mostly for recreation. The Khasi tribe of the region also celebrates the ripening of paddy by dancing around their harvest.

Thoko Gari Cham or the Dance of Skeletons is an interesting twist to the Cham dances that abound in Arunachal Pradesh. Since Arunachal borders Bhutan and Tibet, Buddhist traditions and influences have modified the indigenous culture of the state.

Ngonpae Don literally means the Ritual Dance of the Hunters. The hunters are supposed to represent the bodyguards of the Buddha while the 'Sha Cham' represents the 'Sacred Stag', which is a messenger of Death. The Khamptis, Khampas, Monpas, and Sherdukpens are tribes of Arunachal Pradesh that perform this chase-dance.

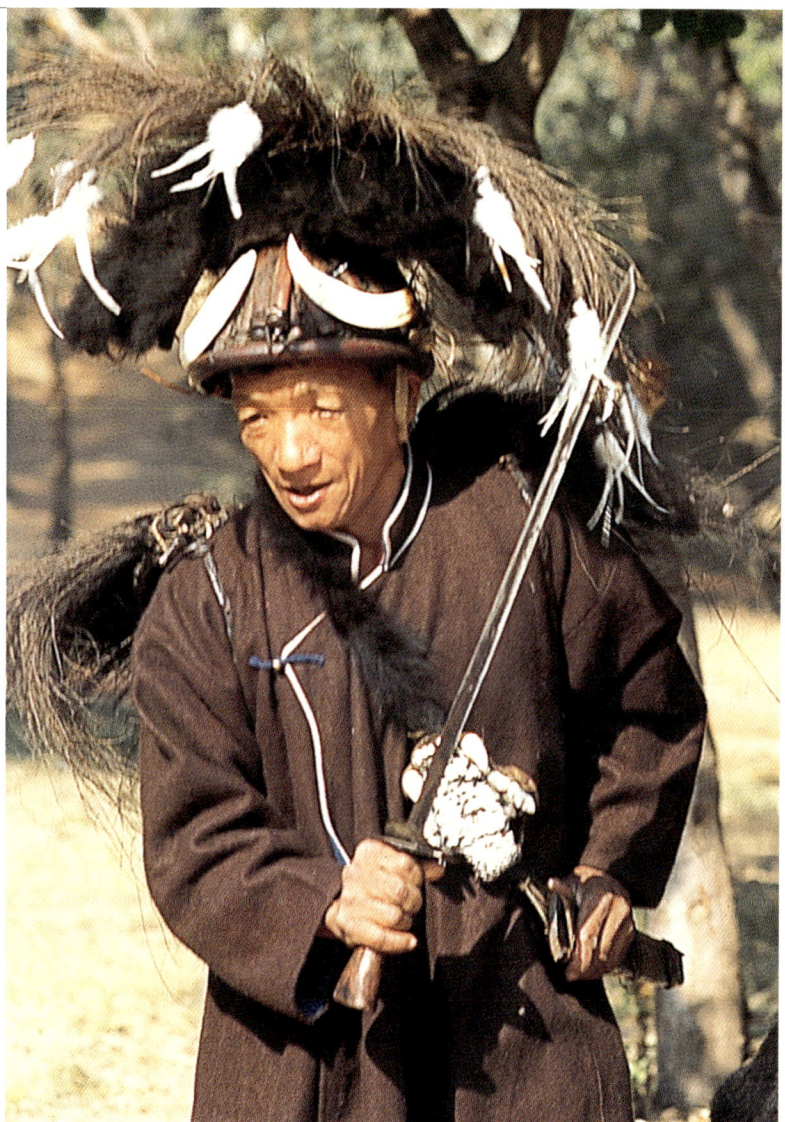

Norms, Means & Ends

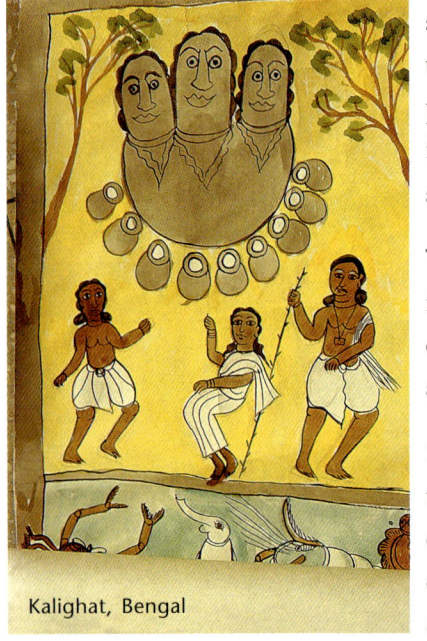

Kalighat, Bengal

While folk dances are full of spontaneity and freedom and convey an impression of unfettered primordial vitality, they are not performed anytime or anywhere. A suitable occasion and an equally appropriate setting are always considered important as per norms. Though unwritten, these norms are nevertheless followed by tradition and practice. Thus, the free will that seems so powerful an element of folk forms exists only within the overall framework of the dancers' social obligations and custom-bound daily lives.

The underlying emotion in all such dances is spiritual joy. Another important aspect is love and its expression through courtship dancing. This type of dance does not connote sexual licence although it certainly allows a free mixing of the two sexes.

Songs that convey either heroism or love are common and a part of the everyday lore of these villagers. These songs find a physical expression in dance. Collective dancing, get-togethers, large-scale celebrations and festivities also help to nurture community feeling and friendship.

As the dancers are mostly agrarian or pastoral people, they have rites (that have evolved through centuries) connected with all events that have significance in their calendar, like harvesting, sowing, reaping, rains, and other seasonal changes. These rites include dances, in which either nature or the gods are thanked for making these events possible or the events themselves are portrayed symbolically. Naturally, activities like planting and winnowing are a part and parcel of their dance depictions.

While most of the dancing takes place in the open, certain ritual dances do call for a special setting – for example, a shrine or a backdrop and props of totemic value. A place consecrated to animistic or tribal deities, as well as masks, paintings, and totems are necessary in ritual dances.

In established ancient cultures, dance is akin to prayer and this is quite true of Indian folk dances too. Dancing is a means of communication with the divinities. At the far end of the spectrum are the performers who are invested with special powers or enjoy hereditary rights to perform certain ceremonies or dances. Shamans and magicians too project their art or vision through these dances. A few dances are meant to ward off evil spirits. Often such dances are frenzied, with the performers apparently becoming possessed

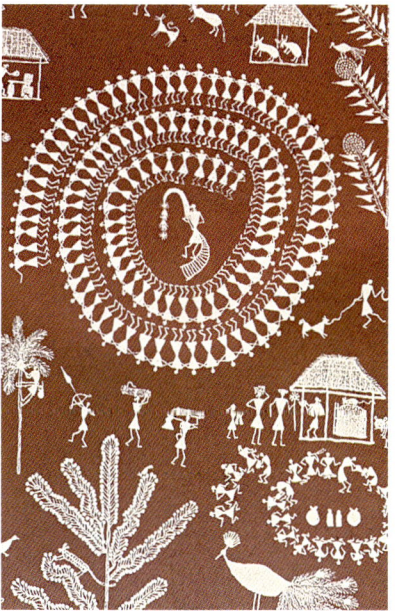

Warli, Maharashtra

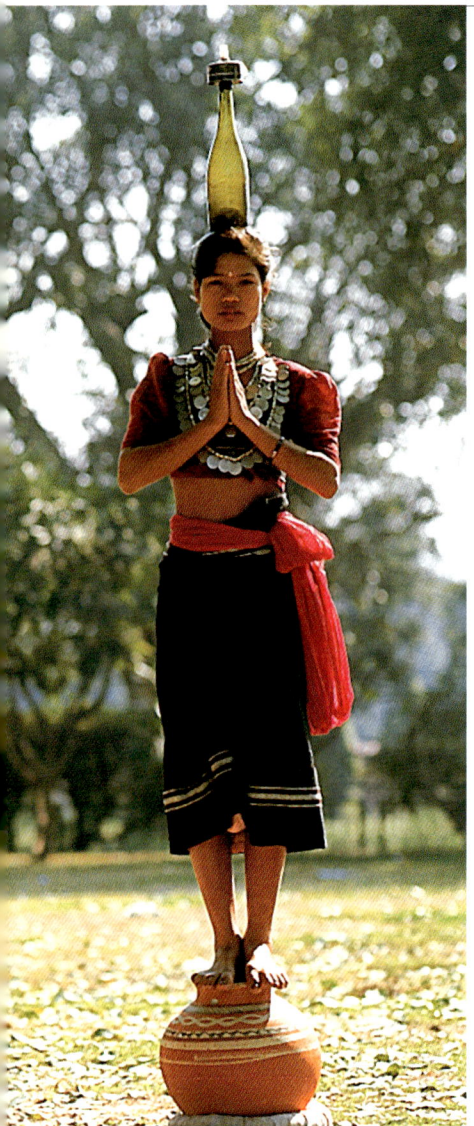

themselves. Sometimes animals are sacrificed during the ritual performance.

When women and men dance together, they usually do so in orderly formations of two separate lines or rows facing each other and moving in harmony. Circular patterns predominate and loud clapping helps to keep the rhythm.

Lots of props are employed in folk dances, from agricultural ones like sickles to ornamental ones like huge floral headdresses. Shields, swords, and spears are used in the martial dances whereas bamboo poles or banana stems are common in ritualistic styles.

Often pots and pitchers or headdresses are balanced upon the head while the hands are left free to make gestures and clap. Feathers and plumes of birds like the fowl and peacock, or belonging to more exotic and rare species are used in costumes or props as a mark of exclusivity.

Hajagiri, Tripura

Costume, Jewellery and Instrumentation

Costume for folk forms are generally derived from the everyday attire of the dancers. Sometimes the outfit is grander than usual and made from expensive material for special occasions like the advent of spring or Holi or Dussehra celebrations. Mostly, folk dancers do not have special costumes just for dancing (as is the case with classical dances) but make do with whatever they possess or are used most sparingly in their daily lives. Special masks and other such props, though, are made for the occasion and, once the ritual is over, destroyed in keeping with the traditions of the particular tribe or society.

Green, red, and yellow are the predominant colours in costume, although pristine white is used too. Green symbolises the agrarian background the dancers hail from, red stands for power and propitiation, and yellow for happiness and springtime rejuvenation. Black is used mostly in dances associated with evil spirits or forces and also in tantric and sorcery-related rites.

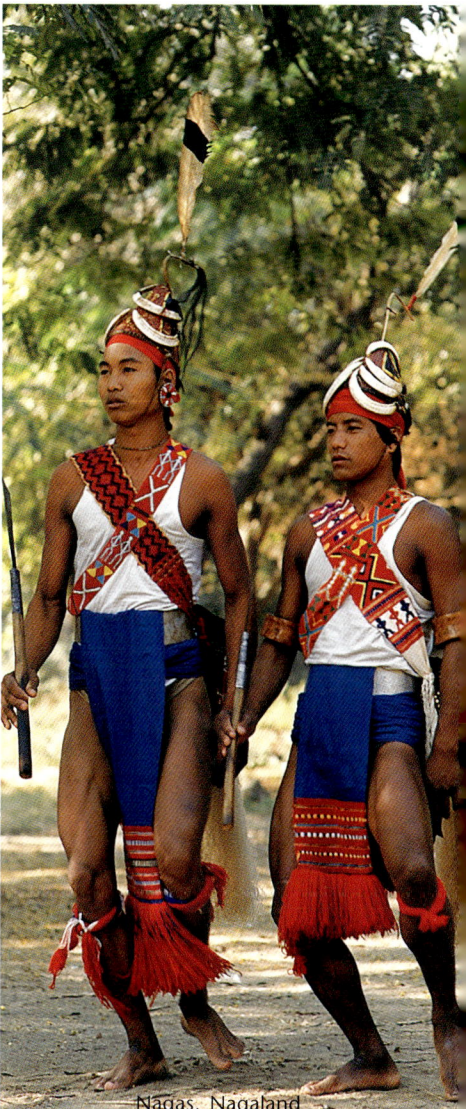

Nagas, Nagaland

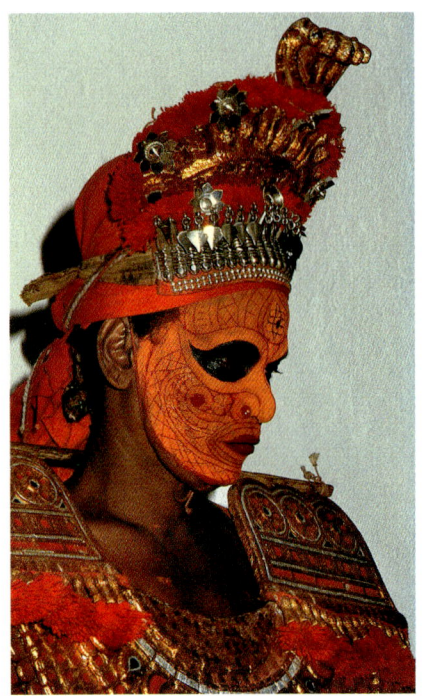

Teyyam, Kerala

Beads, silver jewellery, feathers, plumes, and grass are used either for decoration or for their symbolic value. Banana skin and coconut fibre are frequently used in the southern and eastern India. Mirrorwork and fine embroidery add glamour to folk costume in Gujarat and Rajasthan while the tribal men mostly perform bare-chested and minimally clad.

Ankle bells that resonate with the rhythm are generally indispensable dance accessories. Mostly, brass, copper, and silver bells are used. Where swords and shields are necessary, they are forged out of iron or steel.

Drums of all shapes and sizes play an important part in folk dances and most dancers perform to the sonorous accompaniment of drumbeats. Singing and clapping make up for a dearth of musical inputs in some styles.

While most folk dance forms draw their inspiration from nature and its cycles, a few do show certain interesting variations. The dances of the coastal cultures, for example, reflect those activities that are important to their own trade, such as seafaring and fishing. Similarly, hunting being a vital part of nomadic life, chases and hunts are mimed in their dances.

All folk dancers dance for themselves, caring nothing for audience and applause. Their inspiration comes from nature, from deep-rooted customs or simply, the many impulses of their own hearts, be it foreboding or delight. As such they show themselves to be closely connected to themselves, their habitat, and Mother Earth. All these varied dances are a spontaneous display of joy, unencumbered and unpretentious. The transparent faces of the dancers mirror their inner emotions and their joy touches all. Through the folk dances of India, rural India comes vividly alive in all its grace, bounty, beauty, exuberance, and hospitality. The folk dances of India represent the nation's warm heart and its true soul.

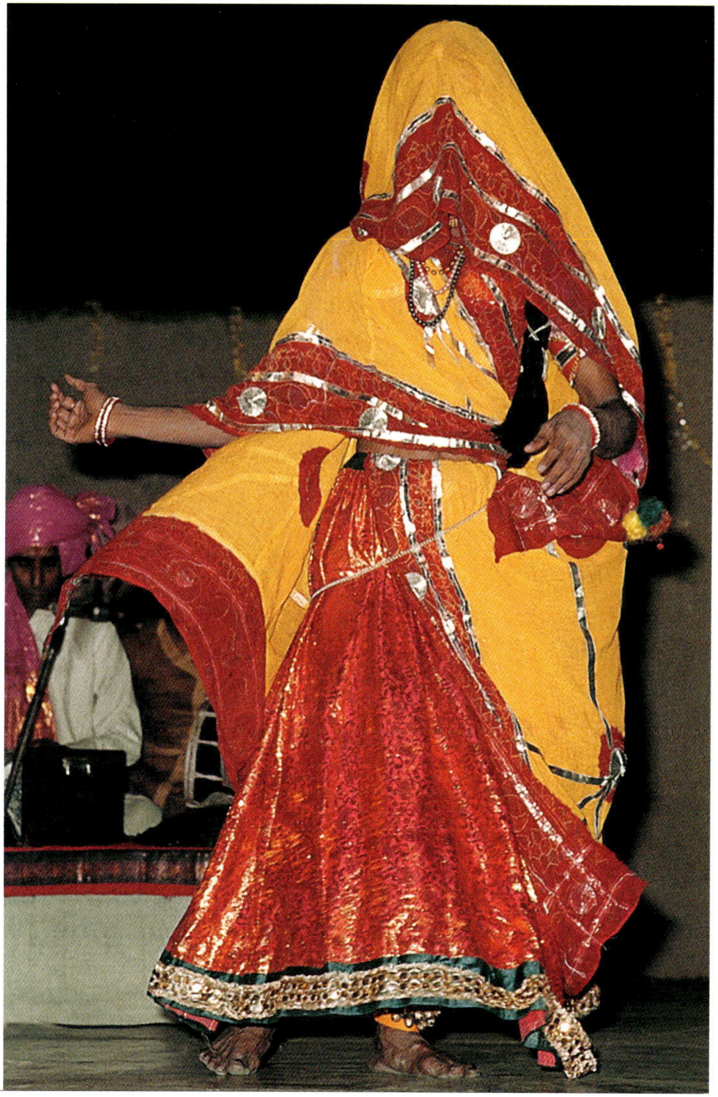

Ghoomar, Rajasthan

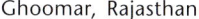

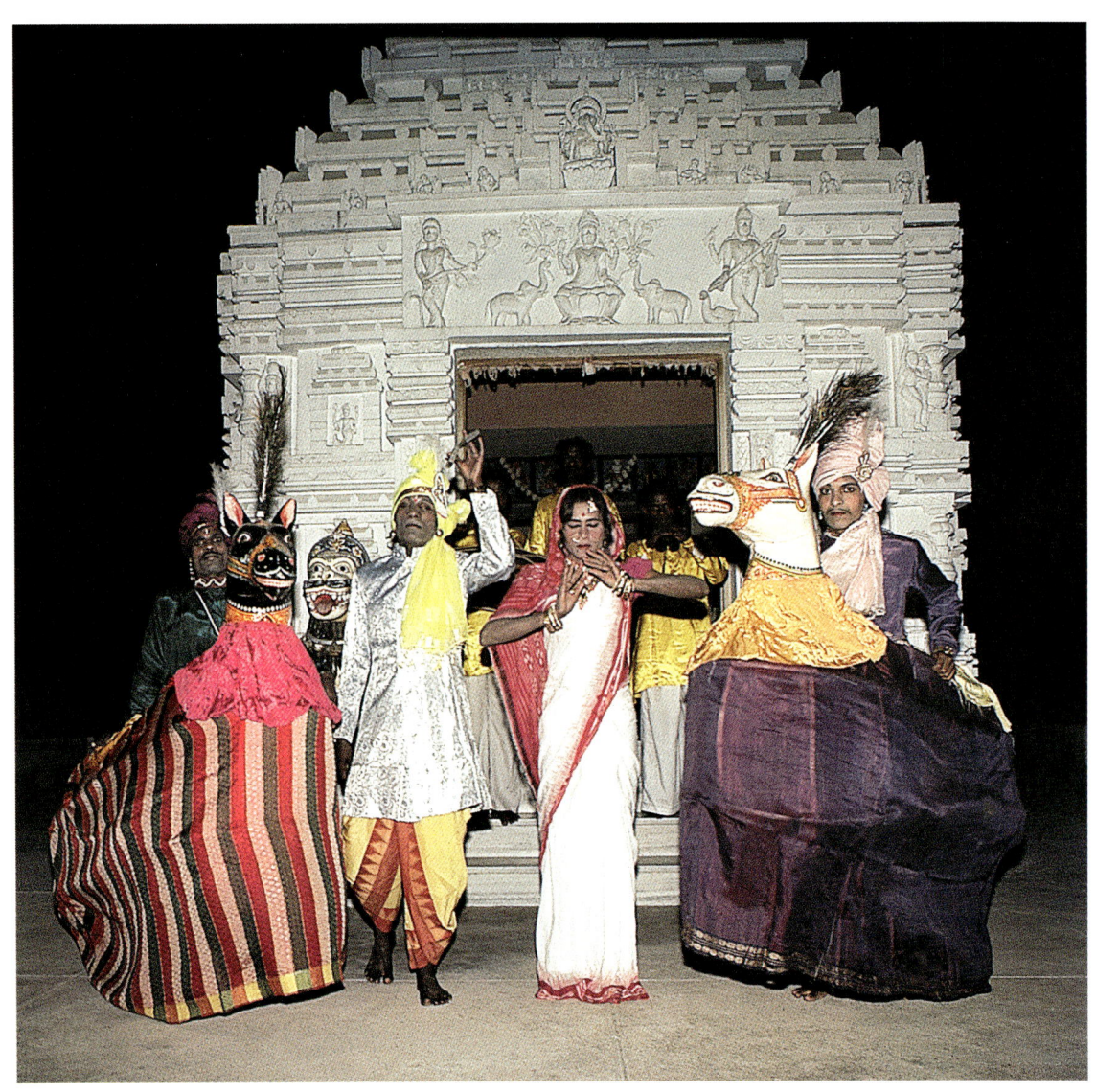

Chaiti Ghori, performed by the fisherfolk of Orissa

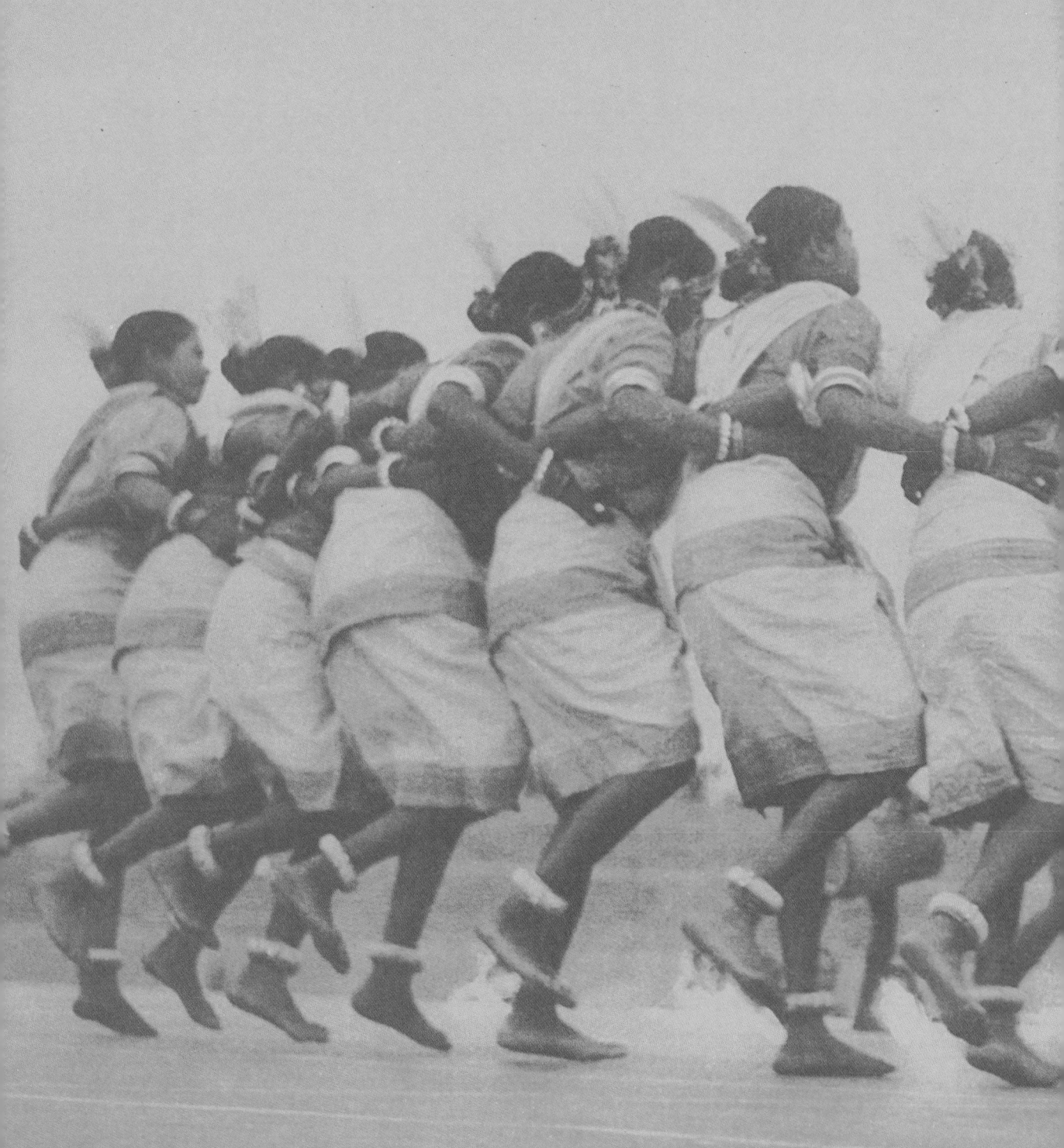